MOCHA & THE BILLIONAIRE'S SON: A BWWM ROMANCE

REGINA SWANSON

Royalty Publishing House is now accepting manuscripts from aspiring or experienced urban romance authors!

WHAT MAY PLACE YOU ABOVE THE REST:

Heroes who are the ultimate book bae: strong-willed, maybe a little rough around the edges but willing to risk it all for the woman he loves.

Heroines who are the ultimate match: the girl next door type, not perfect - has her faults but is still a decent person. One who is willing to risk it all for the man she loves.

The rest is up to you! Just be creative, think out of the box, keep it sexy and intriguing!

If you'd like to join the Royal family, send us the first 15K words (60 pages) of your completed manuscript to submissions@royaltypublishinghouse.com

PROLOGUE

THE CRAZY CHICK

*a*mbrosia was grateful that she worked out five days a week; otherwise, there was no way she would be able to drag this huge hunk of a man down to her basement. She usually avoided chubbier men, but this one here had been persistent. They'd both been at the bar at Champ's Bar & Grill. Ambrosia seriously just wanted to be left alone that night. It'd been a rough day at the hospital. She'd lost one of her patients. Little Malcolm Tatum had been her patient at Children's Medical Center for over a year. Ambrosia really thought he'd made a turn for better and was on track for a full recovery, but last Friday he slipped into a coma. He'd lasted only 5 days. When he died, Ambrosia was devastated. When Chubby came and sat next to her at the bar, she had warned him that she didn't feel like talking and only wanted to enjoy her drink. It was his own fault for driving her back to that dark, violent place that she'd left long ago. As long as Ambrosia took her medications, she could function just as great as any of the other nurse's on staff at the medical center; but if she missed a dose, look out world. She had been so consumed with trying to will Malcolm back into consciousness that she hadn't taken her Abilify or Prozac all week.

Ambrosia sat at the bar wondering if there was anything else that she could have done to save the little boys' life. She tried her best to

1

block the man out, but his persistence won out, and Ambrosia decided to take her anger at losing her patient out on him. He literally jumped at the opportunity to screw her when she suggested they go back to her place. Ambrosia had been done with trifling men long ago. He didn't even ask her name. He followed behind her like a sick little puppy as she sped off, weaving in and out of traffic. She drove in the direction of her house. It would be his last opportunity to come to his senses and escape, but he wasn't having it. He stuck right on her tail, even as she reached speeds of above 100 miles per hour.

When she abruptly swerved the vehicle into her driveway, so did he. She shook her head. That had been easy as pie. *"That's what happens when you think with the little head versus the big one,"* Ambrosia said to the figure in her review mirror.

She got out of the car, briskly walking to her door. He jogged to catch up. As she stuck her key into the lock, he rubbed against her, allowing her to feel how hard his penis had become. She rolled her eyes. He reached under her skirt, sliding his hands into her panties. He roughly stuck his fingers into her vagina, and Ambrosia's body responded. She had no control over the sensation that she was feeling as she moaned. It had been months since she had been with a man. He used his other hand to slide his fingers into her ass. Ambrosia loved it. She stood and allowed him to assault her in two of her most sensual spots. It was rough, just the way she liked it. He leaned down biting her on her shoulder. Ambrosia knew it was risky to be out on her front porch in this position. Any one of her neighbors could look out their window and have a heart attack by witnessing her in the middle of a sex act. She would just have to hope all of their old asses were long gone to bed. Besides dealing with nosey old people, it was a great place to live. She lived in a quiet cul-de-sac. All of her neighbors were elderly retired couples.

As Ambrosia was about to climax, she reached down, unbuckling her assailant's pants. She freed his member from captivity and began stroking it. She would definitely enjoy the length of it before she knocked him out. Ambrosia's body began to shake. After what seemed like ten minutes, her orgasm was complete. Chubby picked her up and stumbled just inside the front door. He used his feet to kick the door closed behind them. Dropping her down on the chaise lounge, he began sliding out of his pants. He grabbed Ambrosia's legs, dragging her ass to the edge of the lounge. He ripped her panties right off her body, something she never thought that was possible. She'd always assumed in the movies that they used break-away panties for rough sex scenes. "*There goes that theory*," she thought.

He was actually really good at sexing Ambrosia. She was enjoying getting freaked by him as he stuck his tongue in every hole that he could find on her body. "*Too bad, you have to die*," she thought.

Once he'd reached his first climax, Ambrosia went into the kitchen to fix them a drink. She reached into her wine rack, opting for a bottle of vodka. She had suggested they take shots, wanting him to quickly ingest the ketamine hydrochloride. Once he did, he would lose consciousness quickly.

Everything went according to Ambrosia's plan. In fact, it worked a little too well. She struggled with the weight of his body as she attempted to move him. Ambrosia began mumbling. She was almost to the basement door of her home.

"But no, your ass wanted to try to get the pussy, talking all that lame shit about how you treat a woman. This motherfucker didn't even have the decency to take off his wedding ring. I hate men like you. All week long, you're the loving husband. Get up, go to work, come home, play with the kids, eat dinner, screw the wife, go to bed, and get up to do it all over again. But then on Friday night, you tell the missus you're going out to hang with the fellows when you're really out looking for a piece of ass. You're out there hunting for the no strings attached pussy. But you motherfuckers better watch out because Ambrosia is hunting y'all's asses now. And I'm playing for keeps."

Ambrosia had finally managed to drag big man to the top of the stairs. She opened the door and pushed him down. He tumbled, arms flailing legs all over the place. His incoherent moans let her know that he was still alive. He could have very easily broken his neck as he went head first down the stairs, and Ambrosia could care less. Her mission was now complete. She took the key from her pocket. Locking Chubby downstairs had caused her to break a real sweat.

* * *

"AMY!"

Ambrosia jumped at the sound of Mocha's voice. She wondered if she had said anything out loud about her past life. Mocha was standing over Ambrosia, clearly waiting on an answer to a question that she hadn't heard.

"I'm sorry. Could you repeat your question?" Ambrosia requested. Mocha looked annoyed.

"For the third time, did you deliver those papers to Mr. Baldwin's office?"

"Yes, indeed," Ambrosia said relieved.

"Great," Mocha replied as she walked back into her office.

"Dammit," Ambrosia spoke after Mocha closed her office door. She refused to be found out by her boss, was determined to keep hidden that she had a secret past that she was running from. Starting over was not something that she wanted to do again. She had just gotten used to her new name, Amy.

Amy looked at Mocha's closed office door. "I won't allow you mess this up for me," she mumbled.

1

MOCHA

*H*e loved the way the water shimmered on her brown skin. He felt like a stalker. His eyes were glued to her body. He knew this was an invasion of her privacy, but he was captivated beyond his senses.

Mocha had just finished her nightly workout. It had become her ritual. She gave 100% to this company, and there was no downtime throughout her day to relax. One of the benefits of being CEO of Baldwin Enterprises was having 24-hour free access to the rooftop gym. It was a haven for exercise enthusiasts. In addition to the latest machines and equipment, it had an Olympic-size pool, sauna, and whirlpool.

Each night as Mocha finished her light weights routine, she would dive into the pool to cool off. This was when her secret admirer would appear. He would sneak in and stand in the same spot behind the juice bar. Rather than being afraid, Mocha was amused. She had watched her boss's son grow into a well-rounded young man.

Mocha thought that he would make some young woman a nice husband one day. If she had been five years younger, she might have even been the one, she thought to herself. But with their age and cultural differences, she never gave it any serious thought. One thing Mocha didn't mind, though, was teasing her admirer.

Tonight she had worn the skimpiest two-piece bathing suit she owned. The bikini bottoms barely covered her ass while the top amplified the pertness of her breasts. The orange color against her chocolate skin made her appear goddess-like.

After swimming 20 laps in the pool, she decided it was time to put on a show. If she were honest with herself, she would admit that she loved being watched by him. It made her long for a man's touch; but with the hours that she put in at work, it left little time to find a decent man, so for now, she would continue with this secret rendezvous of teasing little Billy Baldwin.

Mocha swung her long strands more than needed to release the excess water from her tresses. She slow-walked with an extra sashay to make her ass appear as if it were smiling for his eyes only. When she reached the lounge chair, she spun to give him a clear view of her protruding nipples that stood at attention from the cool breeze flowing throughout the wet area.

With that one simple spin, Billy's erection was attempting to escape his trousers. He wanted her nipples in his mouth in the worst way. It took every fiber of his being to keep from rushing over to her and taking what he wanted. His arousal was at a level that made him think savage thoughts. Her body was the icing on the cake. His initial desires for her began in the boardroom. She was, simply put, the most intelligent woman he knew.

Mocha and Billy had been paired together to work on five acquisitions over the past year. It had been the best year of his life. For once in his life, he had been eager in the mornings to get up and come to his father's company–although it had little to do with learning the inner workings of his dad's company and more to do with spending as much time as he could with Mocha.

Mocha probably thought that he was the dumbest man on the planet. The truth was that he had graduated summa cum laude from Harvard University. He had also earned an MBA from Princeton, and not even his family knew he earned a doctoral degree six months ago from Carnegie University's online degree program. But when he was around Mocha, his brain seemed to go on hiatus. He left every meeting with her feeling like he was 2 years old, based on all the babbling that he did.

Sometimes Billy felt that it was simple infatuation, but at other times, he felt that he wanted more than just a lustful night with her. He could have his pick of any single woman working in his dad's company, and probably half of the ones who were married, but they never held his attention past 10 minutes. Mocha invaded his every thought at just about every minute of the day. His dreams did not even allow him a vacation from fantasizing about her beauty.

Mocha continued to taunt his manhood. As she leaned over to dry her feet, she exposed much of breasts. The only things covered were her nipples. After drying her body, she slipped on a robe and headed towards the showers. She was within five steps of exiting the wet area when she abruptly stopped. She had begun to feel a little adventurous.

Mocha turned towards where Billy thought he was being inconspic-uous. He held his breath hoping he had not been discovered. The last thing he wanted was for her to think he was some type of peeping Tom. Mocha walked with purpose, her sashay of earlier non-existent. With each step that she took, Billy's heart rate increased. When she stopped right in front of him, he held his breath.

Mocha reached up to him, grabbing his head. She pulled his lips to hers as their tongues intertwined, desperately seeking pleasure. Mocha was the first to break away. She stepped back. Billy stepped forward. He tried to reach for her again. She moved out of his reach. She smiled, turned, and walked away.

Billy stood looking confused. Wondering if he was dreaming, he reached down to pinch himself. He yelped from the pain he'd just caused, wondering if he should follow her. She turned, looked at him, and winked; he smiled. Billy decided against following her. His sexual emotions were in overdrive right now. When he had the chance, he wanted to make the softest, sweetest love to her. Right then, at that moment, he would be a raging beast. He knew in that self-controlled instant that he planned to make Mocha his wife.

Mocha laughed at her brazenness when she reached the women's locker room. She couldn't believe she had just done that. It was so out of her character, but she couldn't resist. Billy had been silently stalking her for just over a month now. It was crazy that he thought she couldn't see him. With all the mirrors in there, she had a clear view of him every single night. Her view, in fact, had been of all of him, including his giant erection. A thought hit her: maybe he wanted her to see him. Maybe this was a part of the silly game that he was playing.

"Shit, I just played right into his hands!" she exclaimed. *"Well,"* she thought, *"that won't happen again. There is no way I'm going to get caught up in a nasty little affair with the boss's son."* Mocha had heard all the comments from the women daily, trying to get him to notice them. Some had been so bold as to walk right up to him and grab his crouch telling him exactly what they wanted to do with it, but from what she heard, he hasn't taken any of them up on their offers.

"What if he's gay?" she thought, but hastily dismissed the idea, *"There's no way he would get that hard watching my body if he was into men."* Mocha decided to forgo the steam room tonight; she needed to make a quick stop at the store to pick up something to eat for dinner.

She quickly dressed after getting out of the shower, grabbed her hair, and swiftly wrapped it in a bun. She threw her bag over her shoulder and left the locker room, wondering if Billy had left the building yet. The elevator made a rapid glide down to the parking garage. As she walked towards her car, she noticed a shadow of someone standing next to it. She immediately reached for her mace. She wasn't the least bit afraid. The only way they would get the best of her was if they had a gun. She was confident in her self-defense abilities. Since Mocha chose to live in Houston, Texas, three hours away from her family in Dallas, her dad had enrolled her in self-defense classes to give him peace of mind.

2

BILLY

*a*s Mocha got closer to her car she realized it was Billy. He looked every bit the school boy with his hands stuffed in his pockets. He was also sporting the goofiest smile, yet it appeared cute on him.

"Hi," he spoke when she was within hearing distance. "Hello again," she responded being facetious. Awkward silence ensued. Billy finally uttered what Mocha thought sounded like he was asking her out.

"Excuse me," she replied.

"I HAVE season tickets to the Houston Summer Musicals. I was wondering if you would like to join me for their upcoming show," he responded,

Mocha was impressed. He had done his homework. She absolutely loved musicals. Musical theater had been her career choice up until she reached college, when she decided on a more practical career in business management.

She thought for a moment. She knew the upcoming show "Mamma

Mia" had been sold out for weeks now. She had tried mercilessly to get a ticket, but to no avail.

"I would love to go," she heard herself respond, "but only because I'm a lover of theater, and I suspect you already know that."

Billy held up his hands, "guilty as charged," he responded.

IT WAS Mocha's turn to be embarrassed. Without warning, her stomach let out the loudest growl she had ever heard. Billy smiled.

"I know this amazing French restaurant not far from here," Billy whispered, "we could swing over to grab a bite to eat."

Mocha laughed. She couldn't think of any excuse that wouldn't sound lame, so she agreed. Billy insisted on her riding with him in his car. She wondered if he was being a gentleman or a show off. He had just purchased the new 2016 Lamborghini Aventador. It wasn't even available yet to the general public, but the Baldwin name alone came with a slew of perks.

Billy was into cars, and he talked much of the ride about the new features of the Aventador. Mocha didn't see what the big deal was. His $400,000 car rode no better than her $40,000 Mercedes Benz C class.

Billy decided to take her to Etoile's. It was a little French restaurant that was perfect for romancing Mocha. He had taken a few dates there in the past, but this would be the first time that he was trying to make a good impression.

In less than ten minutes, Billy and Mocha were led to their table. They scanned the menus and quickly ordered. Billy was just about to ask Mocha what she thought about the restaurant when he was interrupted by Erin Goldberg.

Erin also worked at Baldwin Enterprises. She was one of the many single women who had tried to charm their way into Billy's heart. Billy had taken her out once, but was immediately turned off by her constant references to her designer clothes, bags, and shoes. He even remembered her mentioning that she wore designer underwear. Erin kept her eyes glued to Mocha as she talked to Billy.

"I really had a great time the last time we went out, Billy. I'm looking forward to us hanging out again."

Billy didn't respond. He noticed how rude Erin was being to Mocha as she never acknowledged her. He knew Erin recognized her. Everybody that worked at the company knew Mocha; she was the face of Baldwin, the one who greeted the staff every Monday morning on the telecommunications monitor.

"Erin, you know Mocha, right?" Billy had called her out. She had no choice but to verbally acknowledge her.

"Of course," Erin replied. "So are you two putting in some extra hours over a working dinner?"

"NOPE," Billy replied. Mocha smiled at his devious side.

ERIN TURNED BEET RED. She stammered her way through a few more ill-advised questions before turning and retreating to her girlfriends, who were sitting on the other side of the room.

"You are terrible," Mocha stated when Erin was out of earshot.

"SERVES HER RIGHT for intruding without an invitation. She'll think twice before approaching us next time," Billy added.

"Next time?" Mocha questioned.

"I'M AN OPTIMIST," Billy winked at her.

Mocha damn near wet herself. That wink and smile was sexy as hell. She crossed her legs under the table and squeezed them tightly. She was starting to second guess herself for accepting his dinner invitation.

They enjoyed their dinner in silence with an occasional word or two about the tastefulness of their entrees. Mocha had ordered the seared duck with green apple and red bell pepper chutney while Billy enjoyed the braised beef short ribs, celery root mousseline, and fall vegetables. Mocha laughed at his selection of short ribs. She wondered if he really liked ribs or was just trying impress her by selecting a food commonly associated with her culture.

Billy was nervous and didn't want to say the wrong thing. Mocha was nervous that he would flash that sexy smile again and, in turn, wake her libido.

Billy decided that they both needed to lighten up, so he ordered a 1989 bottle of Chateau Latour, Pauillac. Mocha was impressed by his selection. Her dad was a collector of fine wines, and she had given him the exact same bottle as a Christmas gift last year. She knew that the bottle was priced just above two grand.

Mocha was fascinated with little Billy, as she secretly called him. So far, he had done everything right—of course, with the exception of the month long voyeurism that he enjoyed, but even that had made her feel sexy and desirable. The bottle of wine had been just what the two of them needed, and after their 2nd glass, they were both chattering like old friends.

Billy talked of his college days, pledging, and even confided in her that he had earned his PhD. She was the first person that he had told. When she asked why he had not told his family, he replied, "They could care less." He spoke of his graduation when he received his master's degree.

Her heart hurt for him when he said that no one in his family had shown up. A week before, he called to see when they would be flying in. They had totally forgotten. His parents had planned a vacation with friends and didn't want to back out on them. Mocha could tell he still harbored resentment by the way he spoke.

Mocha had never experienced anything on that level from her family. They had all been so tight that it was a given: if someone was having any type of event, they all took part in it. Her aunts, uncles, and cousins had all shown up for something as simple as to help her get ready for prom.

Mocha changed the subject she didn't want her night to turn sour because of something that happened in Billy's past. She talked about her college days. She told Billy how she had spent a year studying abroad in Spain. Initially, it had been awful being so far away from her family and friends, but eventually, she met a family that had taken her in and treated her as if she were a distant relative visiting.

By the time they realized it, they had drank the entire bottle. They had forgotten that Erin was even still in the restaurant. She had her eyes glued to Billy and Mocha's every move. When Mocha happened to glance in her direction, she burst into laughter at the daggers that Erin was shooting in her direction.

Erin was livid. She could not believe that Billy was out in public with Mocha. She seethed at the fact that she should have been there enjoying his conversation as opposed to Mocha.

Mocha turned to Billy and bluntly asked, "Did you screw her or something?"

"Who Erin? Heck no," he replied.

Mocha laughed again. "Heck no," she mocked. The wine clearly had her bubbly. Billy, on the other hand, had only a slight buzz.

"Well she is hot and bothered, and looks like she wants to kick my ass," Mocha slurred.

Billy smiled at her speech. He was glad to see another side to her. In the office, she was all business. Most men had been scared away from approaching her because of her no nonsense personality. Billy was the only one who could see behind her hard exterior, and he wanted to be the one to peel back layer after layer to get to know the person behind the strong personality.

They guessed that Erin had enough as she gathered her things. She and her hurlers decided to make a pit stop at the table before exiting.

"Well Mocha, seems as if you've had a bit too much to drink," Erin implied. Mocha immediately put on her business face and voice.

"Erin, I don't believe I have. I thank you for your concern. And," she whispered, "if I do, I am sure Billy will ensure that I get home safely."

"Absolutely," Billy chimed in. With that, Erin quickly turned and walked out of the restaurant.

"You said I'm terrible, what was that?" Billy asked.

"I couldn't help myself," Mocha answered. "She's been staring over here all night. It's a wonder she was even able to finish her meal. Yes, she has the hot's for you real bad, mister."

Billy's tone became serious. "There is only one woman that I have my eyes set on," he stated as he stared into Mocha's eyes.

The seriousness of his tone sobered Mocha a bit. "Billy," she began, "I can't date you."

"Why," he responded.

Mocha thought for a bit, then replied. "You're my boss's son; we are from two different backgrounds. You're five years younger than I am. Shall I go on?" she questioned.

"None of those reasons are valid," he answered.

"Really, so do you think that your father would be ok with you dating his right hand woman, who just so happens to be black and older than you?" Mocha inquired.

"I stopped caring what my father thought about my choices when I was in 10th grade," Billy responded.

Mocha was speechless for a moment. Finally, she said, "It's getting late. I better get home. I think I'll take a taxi home and pick up my car tomorrow."

Billy was jumping up and down inside. He knew he had aroused her curiosity. It was just what he wanted. He would do everything he could from this point out to woo her. He planned to make her his, no matter what anyone else thought.

"Mocha it doesn't make sense for you to take a cab when I can drop you off. I'll send a car for you in the morning to bring you to work. That will save a lot of time."

Mocha agreed, but she told herself that she was definitely saying goodbye from the car. She would not let him walk her to the door or let him in for a nightcap.

30 minutes later, Billy was walking her to the door. He had insisted. No gentlemen would allow a lady to escort herself to her front door without accompanying her, he had explained. He gently took her keys from her hand and opened the door for her.

"Miss Mocha, thank you for being such lovely company tonight."

He placed the softest kiss she had ever felt on her cheek. Mocha melted, unbeknownst to Billy. She wanted his lips to touch every part of her body. Her nipples stood erect. Billy noticed, but he refused to rush things.

He wanted Mocha in the worst way, but knew he could blow things if they moved too fast. He instructed her to make sure she locked up good. He turned and walked back to his car. Her door was still open. He held up his fingers and mock walked them, telling her to go in and close the door. She did and he drove away.

3

MOCHA

*T*rue to his word, Billy had a driver waiting for her when she woke up the next morning. As soon as Mocha opened her curtains to allow in the morning sun, she noticed the black Lincoln town car. She wondered how long he had been waiting. She didn't want to appear as a diva, so she hurried to shower and dress. She would grab coffee from the cafe in the lobby.

Mocha had to admit, she enjoyed being pampered–last night the five star restaurant, and now being chauffeured to work, it was all so nice. She chided herself for even slightly considering dating little Billy. The driver pulled up in front of Baldwin Towers. He hopped out and ran around to open her door.

Mocha couldn't believe her luck. She was clearly thinking this morning, unlike last night when she taunted Erin. As soon as her feet hit the pavement, Erin appeared.

"Guess you did need a lift last night after all," Erin taunted. "I saw your car in the parking garage."

"Good morning, Miss Goldberg." Mocha's professional demeanor was back in full force. One thing she didn't play with was her employment. Nobody would ever be able to say that she was unprofession-

16

al. As Mocha passed her, she clearly heard Erin mumble the word "bitch." Mocha composed herself before turning around.

"Miss Goldberg, did you say something?" Erin turned and walked away without saying a word. Mocha was furious with herself. This was precisely the reason why she refused to date co-workers. She cursed herself for letting her guard down, even if it was for only a couple of hours last night.

On the ride up to the elevator, she thought of ways to back out of the theater date with Billy. After what had just transpired with Erin, she knew she had to cancel. She needed to stay focused on her career. She had worked her way up from administrative assistant to the boss's right hand, and she refused to let a fling with his son ruin all that she had worked for.

Mocha walked off the elevator. She greeted Amy at her desk and asked her to go back downstairs to get her a latte. After the incident with Erin, she had forgotten to stop at the bistro.

When she walked into her office, she smiled. A huge bouquet sat on her desk. She immediately knew they were from Billy. She knew she shouldn't be, but she was giddy about the flowers. She had thought about him late into the night. Sleep provided her no reprieve as he invaded her dreams.

In her dream, Billy had rang her door bell after she closed the door. When she opened the door, he thrust her against the wall. His ragged breathing against her neck sent chills throughout her body. Some kind of way, her boobs popped out. He hungrily covered her nipples with his mouth. He applied a circular motion with his tongue around her nipples. She reached down to grab his penis. She wanted to feel what she had admired over the past month as he watched her half naked body at the pool.

A knock at the door brought her back from remembering what she had dreamt about last night.

"Hey," Amy called. "Here's your latte. Those flowers are gorgeous aren't they?"

· · ·

MOCHA SMILED AT THE FLOWERS. "Yes they are," she replied.

"LET me know if you need anything else," Amy said before leaving.

MOCHA KNEW Amy wanted to know who they were from, but she would never ask. Mocha had kept everything between them on a business level. She hated blurred lines. She had seen so many relationships ruined by people crossing the line into a so-called friendship, because they had no clue on how to keep work and play separate from each other.

Mocha sat at her desk. She pulled the card from the holder and opened it. It read:

MY DEAREST MOCHA,

THANKS FOR YOUR COMPANY. *You kept me from eating a frozen dinner.*

LOOKING FORWARD TO THE THEATER,

B.

Mocha caught herself smiling after reading the card. She placed it back into its holder and moved the arrangement to the small conference table in the corner of her office.

Mocha felt it. She was falling for him. It had been so long since she had been interested in a man. Up until now, work had been her only concern. She wondered how he was able to sneak past the wall she built up to keep distractions away. Mocha heard a knock on the door. She wondered why her secretary had not used the intercom to let her know what she needed. The door opened, and Billy stuck his head in.

"Hi, your secretary wasn't at her desk, Can I come in?"

"Sure," Mocha replied. Once he was inside her office. She thanked him for the flowers.

"They're beautiful," she told him.

"You're welcome," Billy replied. He asked if she was excited about going to the theater on Friday. They small talked for a few more moments, then he said he had a meeting to get to. He arranged to pick her up from her house at 6:00 pm. He'd take her to dinner first, and then the theater.

Mocha decided to tease him a bit saying, "Will I see you tonight at the pool?"

He flashed that sexy smile and responded, "You just might."

4

ERIN

*E*rin watched as Billy exited Mocha's office. She couldn't believe that Mocha was throwing herself at Billy. There was no way that she was just going to step aside and let Mocha have what she had claimed a long time ago. She had been after Billy for six months before; she had practically begged him to take her out.

"We had a great time too," she said aloud. As she was turning to head back to her office, she saw Mocha's secretary getting off the elevator. Erin's brain started turning. She needed someone closer to Mocha to help keep an eye on her. She figured she had to be the closest person to Mocha that worked here.

Erin greeted Amy and introduced herself. She had seen her many times before, but never spoke because she never had a reason to talk to her. Erin felt that secretaries were beneath her. She felt that way about most of the people working at Baldwin. The only reason she applied for a job there was to get involved with William Baldwin III. She had seen Billy's profile in GQ magazine's issue of most eligible bachelors. Sure, it was taking a little longer than expected, but that was because she hadn't gotten him into bed yet. She knew that once she nailed him in the sack, it would be all over. She would be walking down the aisle within a month. She felt that her lovemaking skills where just that good. All she needed was one opportunity to sex him down, and Mocha would be sent back to the plantation.

Erin had already begun making plans. She wanted a huge wedding. She wanted to invite everyone she had ever met since kindergarten. She would have 12 bridesmaids, both a matron and a maid of honor. Her father would walk her down the aisle. She was deep into her fantasy when she heard the secretary calling her name.

"Oh I'm sorry," Erin replied. "I was lost in la la land. So, do you want to grab lunch today?"

"Who me," Amy beamed.

"Of course you," Erin charmed.

"Sure," Amy replied.

They made plans to meet in the lobby. Erin would drive them to the cafe around the corner. That's where she would start her interrogation. She wanted every piece information she could find out about Mocha. She would figure out how to use it later.

Erin was beginning to think that lunch with the secretary was a waste of time. Amy was acting like chatty Cathy. Erin told herself to stay focused, that having lunch with this woman would benefit her in the long run. All Amy talked about was her freaking dogs and stupid ass cats. When Amy started talking about pooper scoopers, it was time to bring the lunch date to an end. Erin was about to ask the waiter for their check when she thought she'd throw Billy's name out to see if her lunch companion would offer up any tidbits about her boss.

When she said Billy's name, the woman's smile grew 10 feet wide. *"Oh dear,"* Erin thought, *"this woman has a crush on my man too. It seems to me that everybody wants a piece of Billy Baldwin."* Erin decided to put all of her cards on the table. If worse came to worst, she would just deny everything. Who the hell would believe a secretary over me? She was the Vice President of marketing.

"Look," she began, "Billy and I have been secretly dating for almost six months now, but I heard from a reliable source that your boss has the hots for him. I was just wondering if you have seen or heard her say anything about him."

Amy thought for a moment. She couldn't believe Erin had only asked her to lunch to try to get information on Mocha. Then she thought about it, "at least I'll get a little human conversation out of this." She told Erin she hadn't seen Billy or Mocha together at all, but Mocha did get a huge bouquet of flowers this morning.

"Do you know who sent them?" Erin quizzed.

"No, but she did smile really big when she saw the flowers; it was like she already knew who had sent them."

"Do you think you can get a look at that card sometime today?" Erin asked, "maybe take a screen shot of the card with your cell phone?"

"Do you think we can have lunch again here tomorrow," Amy asked. Erin couldn't believe she was being patted down by this woman.

"*Well*," she thought, "*at least she's cheap.*"

"Sure we can do that, and you can tell me what that card said."

Erin paid for their meals. She couldn't wait to get back to the office. It was torture listening to her cackle on about the most boring shit she had ever heard. Amy would be talking about her animals one minute and completely flip, talking about the mailman the next. The one-sided conversation jumped around from various topics every minute. Erin sped as fast as she could on the busy downtown street. She wanted her out of her car as fast as possible. Erin pulled up to the curb in front of the building.

"I can walk with from the garage with you," Amy told her.

"OH NO YOU GO AHEAD. I am taking the rest of the day off," Erin lied.

Amy was wise to Erin dissing her. It didn't bother her a bit. She was happy to finally have a friend at work. She was shunned by almost every other secretary at the company. Most people classified her as weird, but that was all a part of her plan to disappear. No one in Dallas would believe that this 25-pounds heavier, thrift shop-wearing, super nerd was the once brash and sassy Ambrosia.

It was just the way she needed it to avoid prosecution for kidnapping and torching that poor son of bitch who didn't know how to keep his dick in his pants. Ambrosia felt like she was doing his wife a big favor by putting his ass in captivity, but that stupid heifer had installed a damn tracking device on his car. When he hadn't shown up at home after 48 hours, the bitch went into private investigator mode. She tracked his ass right to Ambrosia's driveway.

"If I have to install a freaking tracking device to keep up with my husband, I don't need to be fucking married," she recalled. That little slip up could have landed Ambrosia in prison, but when her neighbor called her to say that her house was surrounded by police squad cars, she hightailed it to Houston. She changed her name, appearance, and profession. Ambrosia hated looking like plain Jane, but for now it would have to do. She would simply have to consider herself eclectic.

MOCHA

*A*my popped her head into Mocha's office. "Hi boss, I'm back from lunch."

NORMALLY AMY WOULD HAVE CALLED her on the intercom to let her know that she was back from lunch, but this gave her an opportunity to see if the flowers were still there. She smiled when she saw them. This would be the easiest task in the world, she thought to herself

Mocha told Amy that she had emailed her a few documents that needed Mr. Baldwin's signature. Amy said that she would take care of it.

"Okay boss, let me know if you need anything else."

THERE WAS a time when Mocha would have taken her forms in to be signed by Mr. Baldwin herself, but after that awkward incident last year, she avoided being alone with him.

Up until that day, she had the utmost respect for the company's owner. Mocha had been working late one night. He came into her office. At first, she thought nothing of it. He was simply making small talk. But when he rounded the corner of her desk and sat atop of it, legs gapped open with his crouch in her face, there was no doubt of his intentions.

Mocha politely stood to move away from him, but he was quick with his hands. In a split second, he had her pinned up against the wall behind her desk. She kneed him as hard as she could. She had hoped to God that she broke something. He squealed like a baby. She watched as he yelled, cursed, and hopped around her office.

When he calmed down, she told him that if he fired her, she would definitely be filing sexual harassment charges against him, and that she would sue the company. From that day forward, most of their communication took place by email, unless something they were working on had cause for them to have an executive conference. In those cases, it was usually a board meeting. The last thing William Baldwin wanted was for his company's name to be tied to a sexual harassment lawsuit. It would kill his profit margin and possible sink any chance of being named a Fortune 500 company by Forbes. As long as Mocha continued to increase his revenue, which clearly she was, he would have to bide his time in getting rid of her.

Sure, Mocha was intelligent and had the balls to bring any of Baldwin's rival companies to its knees, but William felt any number of his top level executives could have rightfully occupied the CEO position. Mocha was named CEO for two main reasons. First, William had gotten wind of several lower level employees threatening to file an affirmative action lawsuit. Secondly, he had a thing for exotic looking women, and he wanted Mocha in the worst way. He had made her CEO believing that she would be so grateful for the promotion that she would open her legs to him. By making her CEO, he was killing to birds with one stone, but that one stone crumbled, leaving him with nothing but disconcertment.

Amy had waited for Mocha to leave the office for much of the afternoon. When she finally ventured from her office, Amy rushed in to open the card.

She read the card and smiled. The card was signed B. "That means Billy," she said. She quickly pulled out her cell phone, took the

BILLY

*M*ocha worked another ten hour day. Her body was screaming for her to jump into the hot tub. She was tempted to forgo aerobics and slide right into the warm bubbly waters. Instead, she decided to cut her aerobics down from an hour to 30 minutes. It was the longest 30 minutes of her day. She hurriedly slipped down into the tub.

Once she was in the warm water, she laid her head back on her towel. Her eyes closed and she was quickly off to sleep. Mocha awoke to the sound of classical music softly playing throughout the wet area. When she looked in the direction of the sound, Billy was there standing next to a table with what looked like food for two.

"What?" she stammered, how long? Where did…" She smiled at his creativity. He was definitely different than the guys she had dated in the past. He walked over to her.

"I was walking by on my way to the treadmill, and I just happened to see you taking up residence in the hot tub," Billy stated. Mocha was embarrassed. She wondered who else had seen her. There was no way he brought all of this up to the roof top himself.

"I figured we shouldn't have a repeat of last night when your tummy started talking to me. The bistro was still open downstairs, so I had them to send up some dinner." He reached down, extending his hand to help Mocha step out of the tub. He grabbed a towel and began to dry her body. It felt too good to Mocha for her to ask him to stop. He started with her neck and worked his way down. She knew that this man was seducing her. Every ounce of her body screamed back, seduce me!

He dried her arms and legs. He had her to sit so that he could dry her feet. She giggled when he dried between her toes. He liked that she was ticklish. Naughty thoughts briefly invaded his brain as he thought of other areas of her body that he wanted to tickle. He mentally chastised himself. He needed to remain focused. He would not rush things with Mocha. If he wanted this relationship to last, he would need to not rush it with physical gratification.

He helped her back to her feet and held out a plush robe for her to slide on. Mocha wondered where it came from. The robes in the locker room were made of terrycloth.

Billy guided her over to the table. He pulled her chair out. She sat. Billy was being the ultimate gentleman, as usual. Mocha was enjoying every minute of it.

As simple as this gesture was from him, it was worth more than gold. The impromptu dinner was something that she was looking for in a mate. Things could never get boring if you spent your life with someone who was creative and spontaneous. When Mocha married, she wanted it to be forever. She wanted the type of love that her parents, grandparents, and sister and brother-in-law shared. Mocha couldn't believe that she was mentally moving his level up. He had now gone from just a date to a potential mate within 24 hours. She was starting to get excited at the possibilities.

They laughed and talked throughout their meal. The conversation came easy for them. They both were surprised at how much they actually had in common. Each had one sibling, a sister. Both their parents had met in college and still remained married to this day. Mocha briefly thought of how his dad had tried to force himself on her. She wondered how many other women he'd done that way. Most perpetrators followed a pattern. If she had to bet money on her not being the first or last, she was confident that she would not lose.

The conversation shifted to what they were each looking for in a mate. Billy wanted someone who was fun to be around. He wanted a wife who he could also call his best friend. Intelligence was important. He wanted kids–lots of kids–but not right away…maybe two boys and two girls. He was getting excited, but stopped himself because he wanted to know Mocha's desires.

Mocha thought for a while. He didn't interrupt. She finally answered. "Love. That's it. Short and simple. I want to feel loved. I want to be the center of my husband's attention."

"Above anything else, love trumps all," she continued,"it's the foundation that will keep a family together." Silence engulfed the room. Each stared burning a hole in the other as their eyes blazed with fire.

"Mr. Baldwin," the worker from the bistro called as he entered the area, "if you all are done I would like to take these things back down stairs so I can lock up for the night."

"Yes, Charles we just finished," Billy told him.

"Everything was wonderful," Mocha stated to Charles as she stood, "I better get changed." Billy watched as she exited. As Charles cleared the table, he commented to his friend, "you've got it bad, and that ain't good."

"I know," Billy responded. They both had been on a quest to find Mrs. Right for the past six months. Unbeknownst to anyone working at Baldwin, Charles was Billy's fraternity brother from Harvard. Charles and Billy decided they were tired of the bachelor life they'd been living. Each had been with so many different women, but none of the women had conversations that convinced them that they were their soul mates. Charles decided to take a different route to finding his Mrs. Right.

Both Charles' parents had died in a car wreck his senior year in college. Upon their death he inherited a chain of luxury car dealerships. He never had to work another day of his life. He was looking for a wife that wasn't materialistic. He wanted his wife to love him for who he was as a person. The only way he knew to find her was to pretend that he was broke. His job at the bistro was his cover story. In all the months of working there, he had not been able to convince a single woman at Baldwin to go on a date with him.

"So what are you going to do about it?" Charles asked.

"I'm going to make her fall in love with me, marry her, and have a house full of babies," Billy stated.

"In that order, huh," Charles laughed.

"That's the plan. She's amazing."

"Have you told your dad?" Charles asked.

"No," Billy responded, "why?"

"Well, based on his reaction earlier when he saw you drooling after her, he may not be so open to having Mocha as a daughter in law," Charles stated.

"I could care less what my father thinks. Mocha is the one. I can feel it."

"That's beautiful," Charles stated.

"Shut up fool," Billy chastised.

"No, I'm serious," Charles said.

"What you're feeling is pure, unadulterated love. It's not clouded by lust because you two haven't had sex yet. I want that," Charles added.

"You'll find her. She's out there somewhere waiting for you," Billy stated.

"But every day it's looking more and more like she is not here at Baldwin. Hell, maybe not even in Houston. I thought that pretending not to be a millionaire was the perfect way to find a wife...but maybe I am being unrealistic. It's been 3 months already," Charles finished.

"Well it's only been 3 months. Why don't you give it at least 3 more months? That's how long it took for me to know for sure that Mocha was the one for me."

Erin had been standing in the wing of the wet area listening to Billy and his friend talk. She had no idea the cook at the bistro was a rich man masquerading as a poor man. He had asked her out on more than one occasion, but she had shot him down instantaneously. She had even gone so far as to tell him that he probably couldn't even afford to put gas in her car. She had been a real asshole to him, but starting tomorrow she planned to wow him. She'd get her rich husband after all. If Billy wanted Mocha then so be it. The cook is sexier anyway, she thought.

Erin tiptoed back out the way she came careful not to let the men see her. She was stoked to hear that Charles really was looking for his Mrs. Right. The women he was encountering just happened to be eliminating themselves from the eligibility pool by sleeping with him so soon. He wanted an old school wife. A wife that respected herself enough not to give up her prized possession without any type of real commitment.

Charles wasn't filthy rich like the Baldwin's, but he had enough money to keep him, his kids, and his grandkids from having to work another day in their lives if they didn't want to. Although he loved the financial stability his parents had left for him, he simply wasn't interested in the day-to-day operations of the dealerships. He let his fathers' best friend handle it. He had earned his MBA at the same time as Billy. He'd worked for several companies just for the hell of it before he decided to open the bistro. When he'd talked to his friend about opening a cafe, Billy was quick to suggest he open it inside Baldwin Towers. Billy had given him the space in the lobby free of charge. Billy figured it was a good investment. His employees no longer had to trudge out to pick up breakfast, lunch, and sometimes dinner.

Charles finished loading the dishes onto the tray. He was exiting as Mocha was walking back through the door. She praised his meal selection once again. She walked over to Billy, and reached up to give him a peck on his cheek. She thanked him for his thoughtfulness.

"You're welcome," he replied.

The awkward silence had returned. Both of them were nervous and wondered if they'd get the chance to really date without being exposed to the drama that usually came along with an office romance. Billy was making it hard for Mocha to stick to her "no dating coworkers" rule.

"What's going on with us?" she asked. Mocha wanted to get everything out to in the open.

She wanted to know his intentions. Billy smiled; he was used to her no nonsense approach in the board room. Now he knew it also extended to her personal life as well.

Although he wasn't ready to reveal his true desire to make her his wife, because he didn't want to scare her off, he did feel like she deserved an explanation.

Billy immediately started to stutter. It was the one flaw in his being that he hated. He didn't stutter much, but when he was intimidated, it reared its ugly head. Mocha intimidated and excited him both at the same time.

"In all honesty, I'd really like to get to know you better on a more personal level. I love everything about you," he stated. Mocha hadn't a clue that would be the response she would receive. She knew he had a little crush on her, but mostly took him as just a big flirt.

Mocha still wasn't convinced that Billy had good intentions where she was concerned. Everything in her screamed he's the one, but years of broken promises from ex-boyfriends had her leery of him. He was different in many ways from the men she was used to dating, but she was convinced that, after the honeymoon stage was over, all men were generally the same—her mother and sisters' husbands being the exception to the rule. Could she trust that Billy would be another exception to the rule? She wondered which half of the pile Billy would fall on: Honest and loving or lying and hateful.

Mocha's mind drifted back to Davis. He had been her everything. When Mocha loved, she loved hard. She was an all-in or nothing type of girl. When she met Davis, she swore to her family that he was the man of her dreams. He was perfect in every way. His only flaw had been that he worked long hours and had weekly business trips out of town. She'd only been able to see him during his lunch hour, on Wednesday nights, and every other Saturday night. It was a weird work schedule, Mocha agreed, but one that she had become accustomed to. She cherished each minute they were able to spend together. After six months of dating, the talk of marriage started to creep into their conversations. Mocha couldn't remember if she was the one to bring up the idea first or if it was Davis.

Although he had yet to make it official by asking her or placing an engagement ring on her finger, she, her mother, and her sister had begun planning for her big day. They shopped for dresses, picked out the cake, and visited wedding venues. Mocha was living the life she dreamed of as a little girl. She was having a whirlwind romance, and Mr. Right was sweeping her off her feet, but it all came to a screeching halt when she visited her gynecologist for her annual well woman's exam.

Within ten minutes of her visit, her doctor had given her the best news she thought possible. Mocha was five weeks pregnant. Mocha thought that things were a bit out of order becoming pregnant first and getting married second but children had been a part of the plan all along. Davis had told her he definitely wanted to have children. Later that evening is when her heart was shattered into a million pieces. Once she told Davis that she was pregnant, he came unglued. He accused her of trying to trap him by getting pregnant on purpose. He called her stupid and yelled that she just had to mess up a good thing by being selfish. Mocha was stunned and couldn't understand where all of his hostility was coming from until his next statements.

He told Mocha that he was married. Davis went on to tell her that he'd married his high school sweetheart almost ten years ago. He told her about his three children aged 8, 4, and 10 months old. He accused Mocha of deliberately trying to break up his marriage. Mocha asked him if was high. "How the hell can I break up a marriage that I knew nothing about?"

"You're a liar," he replied, "every woman knows that if a man doesn't make himself available to you 24 hours a day, he has another family, or he at least has another woman," Davis belittled. Mocha now felt foolish for never questioning his whereabouts. She didn't know there was a need. Davis told her that he would go in half with her on an abortion. Mocha told him to kiss her ass and to get out of her apartment. It was the last time she saw or spoke to Davis.

Mocha felt that everyone was against her. Every person she told about the situation wanted to know how she could have missed the signs that he was married. Mocha was tired of explaining to them that she trusted him to be where he said he was going to be. She didn't think that she was dealing with a five-year-old child.

Mocha assumed that either God was against her too or the stress was just too much for her little baby to handle, because ten weeks into the pregnancy, she miscarried. One month after that, against her parent's wishes, she was heading down Interstate 45 where she planned to start anew in Houston.

Mocha turned to walk away from Billy as a lone tear escaped her eye. She hadn't thought about Davis and the pain he'd caused her in years. Billy, with his easy going and thoughtful spirit, had brought back the memory of that pain. While he seemed nothing like Davis, fear had her heart in a vise grip and wouldn't let go.

Billy had seen the tears in Mocha's eyes as she drifted away from him mentally. He wanted to pull her into his arms, but knew she needed time to process her thoughts and his words

7

ERIN

*E*rin chose the sexiest dress that she could find in her closet to wear to work the next day.

"Let the games begin," she whispered.

She walked in to Baldwin Towers with the confidence of a super-hero. She felt like she had more power between her legs than wonder woman, batgirl, and cat woman all rolled into one. She strutted through the atrium, turning the heads of every single man within eyeshot. She knew all eyes were on her, and she dared not disappoint. She tossed her long blond hair and pursed her lips slightly, sliding her tongue across her upper lip.

"Damn," she heard one the men blurt as she walked past him. She chose to reward him with a backwards glance and a wink. He nearly dropped his cup of coffee.

Erin knew she was a bad bitch. She had the looks and the body to go along with it. Her 5'10" slender frame made her sized C cups look bigger than they were. With just the right bra, they could easily pass for size D. Although her ass was small, the round plump shape caused many a man to drool.

"Bingo," she stated. She spotted her target as she was halfway across the atrium. She knew he had spotted her as well by the huge grin that spread across his face. She walked to the front of the line. The employee's waiting in line quietly grumbled. They were pissed that she cut in front of them but dared not speak up. Everyone had seen Erin when she was on her war path. They wanted no part of her craziness.

Erin stood at the counter. The young woman working the counter stumbled through asking Erin what she would like. Erin stood there rudely, not saying a word and causing tension to spread throughout the bistro.

Charles was amused. He stood eyeing Erin as she put on her show for him. He couldn't deny she was sexy as hell. He imagined her long legs wrapped around his body as he pummeled deep inside her walls.

Erin continued to ignore the poor woman working at the counter. Her eyes were glued to Charles. She wanted no mistake to be made. She was calling him out the only way she knew how. She held a PhD degree in seduction. Everyone in line sighed and huffed, waiting for her to place her order. Most of them were on a tight schedule and didn't have time for her battiness. A few of the customers decided to forgo their morning Java. They didn't have time for her rudeness. Charles finally decided to intervene as to keep from losing any more customers. He walked over to Erin. Awkward was a feeling he hadn't felt in a long time. Erin's stare was blazing hot. It screamed fuck me right here, right now, in front of God and everybody. Charles believed that if he asked her she would do just that. Normally, this type of behavior turned him completely off, but coming from Erin had made it alluring. She oozed sex appeal. The counter separating them and providing a shield was his confidant at the moment. Without it, she and every other customer in line would know the effect she was having on him.

How may I be of service to you today?" Charles asked.

"I want to ride your dick like it's the last bit of pleasure that I will receive before I pass into the afterlife," Erin declared.

The counter girl turned fifty shades of red! She couldn't believe the words that had just escaped Erin's mouth, and neither could Charles. He was thankful that none of the customers could hear her, but he was sure they had a good idea of what she wanted by her body language.

He stood speechless. It was the exact response that Erin knew she would generate. She reached into her low cut shirt pulling out a piece of paper. She had already scribbled her address on it. It also had the words meet me at 7:00 pm written on it. Erin didn't wait for a response. She spun on her heels and put on her closing statement with each sway of her hip. There was no need to turn to see if he was watching her walk away. She knew he, along with every other person standing in that line, was watching her ass jiggle away.

"Damn," a woman in line finally stated, "I'm not even a lesbian, but I would fuck the shit out of her." Every one turned to look at her in disbelief. She responded, "Just saying."

Someone else yelled from behind, "can we get some coffee now?" Charles apologized to his customers and gave them all their coffees free of charge.

8

MOCHA

*M*ocha walked into her office at her usual time. Although she hadn't slept much at all last night, duty called. She was never the one to mope about throwing her own "pity" party. The pain of what she went through with Davis hadn't revealed its ugly head in years. She wondered why, now, her past demon wanted to rear its ugly head. Mocha had tried hard to put everything associated with Davis behind her. He wanted nothing to do with her, and she obliged him.

Often, she thought of the baby they had created. A baby that she thought was created out of love, but in actuality had been created out of one man's lack of self-control and discipline to remain faithful to God and the vows he had promised. Davis was indeed a certified asshole. Mocha was blinded by her own desires of finding that happily ever after.

Without realizing it, Mocha placed her hand on her stomach rubbing in circular motion as if her baby was still in her womb. Mocha would never forgive herself for allowing Davis to cause her so much pain. The weeks after the miscarriage had been the most unbearable. She had fallen into a deep depression that she didn't ever think she could crawl out from, but with help of her parents and sister, she was able to make a full recovery–or so she thought until yesterday.

The words that Billy spoke to her jogged the memory of every single detail of her breakup with Davis. Billy had no clue how broken she had become behind another man. Mocha vowed to never make the same mistake twice. She was an all-in or nothing type of girl. She loved hard, always had. With Billy it would be no different. She didn't trust herself to love a little and keep it moving. She had to protect her heart. A romance with Billy wasn't a chance she was prepared to take to find out if he was her soulmate. The consequences could prove to be too much for her to stand.

"Good morning beautiful," Billy said, as he walked into Mocha's office carrying two cups of coffee from the Bistro.

Mocha didn't respond. Billy felt the tension in the room. He'd hoped that a good night's rest would have helped Mocha get back to her relaxed state after their conversation the day before. Billy closed the door. He walked over to Mocha, sitting both cups on her desk. He silently walked around her desk. Reaching down, he gently pulled Mocha to her feet. He stared into her eyes, feeling every ounce of her pain. The pain he knew had been caused by some jerk. He wanted to know who had damaged her heart. Ultimately, he felt it didn't really matter. His goal was to mend it back together with patience, love, kindness, and simply making all Mocha's dreams come true.

Billy pulled Mocha into an embrace. Initially, she stiffened. Billy wouldn't release her. After a few more minutes, she relented and fell into the embrace. Mocha laid her head on his chest. She loved the way he felt. She loved the way he smelled. He was a masculine man oozing with testosterone. She was falling into the moment.

Billy allowed his hands to slowly roam her back as he massaged the tension from her body. Mocha loved it. Small, unintelligible sounds began to escape her lips. His hands moved up to her neck. He applied slight pressure. His hands continued working as if he was a certified masseuse.

Mocha finally pulled back. She needed to look into Billy's eyes. She needed verification that he was real. She needed to see his intentions. She always remembered her grandfather's words: "The eyes don't lie." What she saw in Billy's eyes gave her chills. There was a softness that couldn't be explained. She saw love. She saw passion. In that moment, she wanted him. She needed him. Billy felt what she saw. He leaned down. He wanted to taste the sweetness of her lips. Mocha moved closer. She wanted his kiss. Their lips had just begun to intersect when her office door flew open.

Mocha's secretary had burst through the door without warning. Instinct caused Mocha and Billy to jump taking steps back away from one another as if they were two kids caught in an inappropriate act.

"Oh," Amy responded, with a smirk on her face. "*Erin is going to love this*," she thought. "I'm sorry, I didn't mean to interrupt. I didn't know you two were in here. I was just dropping off a few packets that need your signature."

Billy and Mocha remained silent. Amy walked over to Mocha's desk. She looked at them from her peripheral vision. She was dying laughing on the inside. They had the dumbest look on their faces, she thought. She placed the file on the desk and walked towards the door. Before leaving out, she couldn't resist.

"Carry on," she retorted as she closed the door.

Mocha was livid. She had every mind to fire Amy's ass on the spot. Over the past two years since she had been her secretary, not once had she walked into her office before calling her on the intercom or knocking on the door; so why today of all days had she decided to break protocol? Mocha sensed that there was more to her just not realizing that she was in the office. Mocha's doubts were starting to creep back in. Billy could see it written all over her face.

"Mocha, please don't let what just happened turn you away from me. I promise we won't let anything like this happen again in the office. It was my dumb mistake. I should have never kissed you here in your office," Billy pleaded.

Mocha smiled, despite the current situation. Billy really was a sweetheart.

"You're smiling. That's a good thing, right?" he questioned.

"That's a very good thing, Mr. Baldwin," Mocha answered. She walked behind her desk. She had just realized how attracted she was to Billy. They definitely needed to keep their distance from each other while they were at work.

"So we are still on for Friday?" Billy asked. Mocha made him stew for a few minutes before answering.

"Yes," she finally stated.

9

CHARLES

*C*harles was starting to get pissed. Billy noticed his friends' reaction as he laughed uncontrollably.

"I'm sorry man. It's just that, in all the women we've been with that we know are certified gold diggers, you think Erin Goldberg could be the one," Billy explained. "Erin," Billy questioned again

"Yeah, threw me for a loop too," Charles answered.

"So what's the plan, Billy asked?

"That's why I called you. You're the one with all the master plans."

"Ok buddy I'm on my way down to your office," Billy stated.

Charles sat in his office waiting for Billy. He needed him to come up with a plan that would keep him from sleeping with Erin before he had gotten a chance to know her. Charles was emphatic about not, once again, putting the cart before the horse. The feelings that he had earlier when Erin was putting on her show was something he hadn't felt in a long time.

Charles wanted Erin in the worst way. Everything that she did this morning had turned him on. Sure, he had been with tons of women— women who defined the word sex goddess to a tee. But today, watching her seduction had him weak in the knees. He needed his friend to help him put things into perspective. Billy could always size up a situation with the utmost ease.

Charles' mind was telling him to sex Erin crazy, and then kick her to the back of the line, but his heart was causing all kinds of friction.

"Where the hell are you Billy?" Charles barked.

"I'm right here," Billy responded, "what's up with you?" Billy was trying to decipher the look on his friend's face.

"Don't tell me you fucked Erin already," Billy joked.

Charles sighed, "Ha, ha, very funny."

"What's the problem?" Billy questioned.

"I don't know if I want to screw her just yet," Charles admitted.

"What's wrong? Are you sick? Where's my friend?" Billy laughed. Charles kept a straight face.

"Oh this is serious," Billy responded as he pulled up a chair to take a seat, "start at the beginning."

Charles told Billy the entire story about what happened with Erin and how his body responded to her. This was the first time Charles had been aroused by a woman since his sophomore year in college. Charles had screwed so many girls and women in high school and college that, by his second year in college, sex was nothing more than an act he participated in.

When Erin evoked this feeling of lust in him, it was either a miracle or God was sending his soul mate to him. Either way he was afraid of the outcome.

Billy couldn't hold it in any longer. He burst into a fit of laughter. Leaning over holding his stomach, he tried to speak.

"So glad that I can amuse you," Charles retorted.

"Really dude," Billy cried out.

"She gave me her address and told me to come over tonight," Charles said, "what do I do?"

"Take your ass to her house," Billy answered.

"No shit. I mean after that. I can't sleep with her. Not yet, Charles stated."

"Ok listen, call the florist. Send her some flowers and on the card say that you want to meet her at some restaurant. Have dinner, and when it's time to go, tell her that you have to get back to the bistro for a shipment. Tell her that it was the only time they could deliver, but that you really wanted to get to know her so you didn't want to cancel. Have a car waiting to take her back home. Apologize and be on your merry way. If she's the one, you'll know by the end of dinner."

"Brilliant," Charles exclaimed.

Charles did just as Billy had instructed. Now he wondered if his friends' advice had been the best approach. He had been sitting in the private dining room at Uchi's for about 45 minutes waiting for Erin to Show. His personal coordinator had come in for the 3rd time to see if she had arrived. Each time he felt more foolish. Charles was about to get up and call it a night when Erin rushed into the room looking frazzled.

Charles immediately stood and crossed the room to her.

"Hi," she breathed. Erin stood there looking a hot sweaty mess. She clutched her purse under one arm and her shoe with a broken heel under the other.

"Are you ok?" Charles asked.

"I'm not, but I will be now that I am here," Erin answered.

"What happened?" Charles questioned.

"Well, I worked over in the south wing today," Erin began. "I didn't get back to my office 'til almost 6:00. That's when I saw the flowers that you sent and the card asking me to meet you here at 7:00. I didn't want to keep you waiting but I really wanted to shower, change, and make myself presentable. On my way here, I had a flat. I was all set to get out and change the tire, but when I looked in the trunk there was no spare. So I did what any other woman would who doesn't want to stand a guy up on their first date. I walked."

Charles was floored. Most women would have called it a night.

"I didn't have a phone number for you to let you know what was going on, and I didn't want you to think that I stood you up," Erin huffed.

Charles was amused but dare not laugh at her. He'd seen how she could behave when she felt slighted.

"I apologize," Charles stated. "I should have given you my contact information just in case you couldn't make it."

The personal coordinator popped back in and asked if we were ready to have dinner. She must have seen the hostess escort Erin into the room.

"I'd like to freshen up first," Erin insisted.

"Absolutely ma'am," the coordinator replied.

Erin stood in the bathroom, exhausted. She admired herself in the mirror. Even after walking two miles out in the Houston heat, she still looked gorgeous.

"This had better be worth it!" she exclaimed. "*Let's snag this man*," she thought as she walked back into the dining room. Charles was standing by the window admiring the landscape. He smiled as she entered.

"You're absolutely stunning!"

"Thank you, you aren't so bad yourself," Erin countered. They both chuckled.

Erin was blown away by how handsome Charles was. She couldn't believe she had been overlooking him for Billy. His ruggedness was turning her own quickly. His unshaven beard was the ultimate sex appeal. His dimpled chin gave a boyish look. He definitely had the bad boy image working. His green eyes matched hers.

"*What beautiful babies we'll make*," she thought.

"Would you like something to drink?" Charles asked.

Erin didn't answer. She just stared at Charles with look of lust in her eyes. Charles knew the look all too well, but he didn't want to take her just yet. If she was the one, he didn't need it to be clouded with sex first and getting to know you later. It was a recipe for disaster.

Before Erin could make her move, the door opened and the waiter brought in their meal. Charles breathed a sigh of relief. Charles stirred the conversation throughout the meal. He wanted to know everything he could about Erin. She was an only child who grew up in Boston. She hated the weather there, so as soon as she graduated high school, she hightailed it down south to the University of Miami, where she earned her bachelor's and master's degrees in marketing. Living in

Miami became a drag, so she picked up and landed a job in Houston at Baldwin Enterprises. Her parents still lived in Boston and tried to get her to move back there every chance they got. She visited them once a year during the holiday season, and they visited her once a year during the summer. Charles kept most of the conversation focused on Erin. Each time she asked a question he would direct the question back to her. Erin knew exactly what he was doing. She obliged, knowing his angle.

Dinner was over, dessert was served, and Erin was ready to make her move. She knew all it would take was one stroke of her tongue down his shaft, and he would be begging her to spend the rest of her life with him.

Erin was sick of the conversation. Without a doubt, she wanted Charles inside of her. She was ready to seal the deal, but before she could make her way over to him, his phone rang. She thought that it was rude as hell for him to excuse himself from the table to take the call. She wondered if it was another woman. A tinge of jealousy engulfed her. Something so trivial usually didn't bother her, but tonight she had been on a mission. She had walked like she was training for the Olympics to make sure this night happened. Charles walked back to the table and apologized, saying he had to get back to the bistro. Apparently, there had been a mix up with a delivery and no one was there to receive it.

Charles was playing the night out just as Billy had told him. Charles could feel the estrogen permeating from Erin's body. He was trying his damnedest to keep his own testosterone in check. When he felt himself slipping and gazing into her green eyes, imaging her lips wrapped around his head, he knew it was time to put a little distance between them. Erin was pissed, but kept the cool girl stance. She didn't want to scare him off. She calmed herself by counting backward from 10 to 1. It was a technique her therapists had taught her when she was mandated to take anger management classes. Those classes had come in handy over the years. The techniques she learned helped her to stay sane and not land her back before a judge over the last 8 years.

Erin hadn't told Charles the entire truth of why she decided to leave Miami. It was a part of her past that she would just as soon forget. Miami held a thunderstorm of not so pleasant memories dating back to her freshman year of college, and pretty much lasting until the day she packed up her car with everything she owned and moved across the country to Houston, Texas. So far, Houston had been good to her. She hoped it would continue to get better in the form of her dinner date, the secret millionaire. Erin smiled, thinking about Charles and Billy trying to make everyone believe that he was just a worker at the bistro.

"Erin," Charles called. She had gone off into deep thought.

"I have really enjoyed spending time with you. Would you please consider joining me again? I'd like to take you out to make up for cutting our evening short. I'll even let you pick the time and place," Charles implored.

Erin stood and walked over to Charles. "My choice, right?"

"Absolutely," Charles responded.

Without warning, Erin reached out and grabbed Charles' crouch. With her free hand, she reached up pulling his lips to hers. Charles' body responded with ease. He burned for Erin, but held his composure. He loved the softness of her lips. It was a stark contrast to the strong hold she had on his penis. Once she released him, she stood back admiring her ability to arouse him. She was indeed pleased with his size.

"Next Friday, my place. Same time. You have the address." Without another word, she picked up her purse and left the room, throwing a slight glance back over her shoulder. Charles smiled; he loved Erin's confidence. He was definitely moving her to the top of his very short list of potential mates.

ERIN

*E*rin was pleased with how the night progressed. She didn't get Charles into bed, but she had definitely left a great impression on him, "otherwise he wouldn't want to see me again," she smiled.

"I'm sorry Miss, did you say something?" the driver asked.

"Not at all," she answered.

Erin spent the majority of the ride daydreaming about her and Charles. She felt she was long overdue for a good romance.

"Home sweet home," the driver said. He opened the door to help Erin out of the car. "Would you like for me to see you in," he asked.

"No I'm fine. This is a pretty safe neighborhood. I'm fine. I am going to walk over to check my mailbox. Thank you."

The driver pulled off, waving to Erin as she walked to the community mailboxes. It was one of the things she hated about living in a condominium. The simple luxury of getting you mail delivered to your door was something that she missed. Most of the mail had been junk besides a few bills. Erin locked the box and began walking towards her unit. Suddenly, the night sky seemed a little darker. The cool breeze whipping against the bushes made sounds that would cause anyone to get a little paranoid. Erin decided to pick up her pace. Out of the corner of her eye, she saw a figure move from behind a parked car. Her heart-beat quickened as the shadow appeared to move in her direction.

"Shit!" Erin thought, realizing she didn't have anything in her hand to use as a weapon. Erin looked over her shoulder to see someone with their head covered with a hoodie. They were approaching quickly. She had the keys to her apartment in her hand. She prayed this person wasn't coming after her. She had taken the utmost care in protecting her privacy. She wondered if her ex-boyfriend had somehow tracked her down to exact revenge for breaking up his marriage to his high school sweetheart. When Erin left Miami, she was seeking to start over in a new city, but she was also running from death threats. After all these years, she didn't want to have to pack up and find another home, especially when she had just found her potential husband.

What happened all those years ago hadn't been her fault, but she was the one suffering. Erin and her college sweetheart had a very tumultuous relationship. Initially, she thought she had found the love of her life. Kane had been sweet and kind throughout their first year of dating. He played football. She was a cheerleader. She gave herself completely to him. Whatever Kane needed, Erin tried her best to supply. Even back then, Erin was looking for her rich husband. Kane's family dabbled in the oil industry. Money was flowing for them. Kane was the typical spoiled rich kid, used to getting his way.

When he picked Erin to be his girlfriend, she was elated. Her entire world began to revolve around him. She let her own grades slip while she did everything she could to ensure that he passed his classes. After sophomore year, Erin was placed on academic probation and kicked off the cheer squad. She was humiliated. When Kane found out what happened, he belittled her. He called her a stupid fuck up. He was adamant in stating that if she couldn't handle being his girl and going to school, then maybe she should just drop out so that she could focus on him completely.

Erin quickly got herself back on track. She would spend all night completing her and Kane's class assignments. She pulled her grades back up to average. She missed cheering, but there was no way that she could keep up with school and cheer. Erin told herself she was doing the big girl thing by focusing on her and Kane's future. She believed that with all her heart. The next few years of college flew by with little fanfare, but senior year, just before graduation, was when her world came crumbling down. Kane changed the locks to his apartment and refused to see her. He had all her things delivered back to her dorm room.

Kane refused to even speak to her. It was his best friend that finally enlightened Erin to what was going on. Kane had another girlfriend. They'd been together since high school. She had gone to another college, but they'd never broken up. She was coming down to Miami for Kane's graduation, where he planned to propose to her. A devastated Erin came unglued. It was then that her anger issues developed.

Up until graduation day, Erin stalked Kane. She burst all the windows out of his car, including the front and back windows. Kane was pissed. He was looking for her to kick her ass. Each night, she stayed at a different friends' dorm room to keep him from catching up with her. On another night, she went to his apartment, throwing several bricks through his windows. By the time he made it outside, she sped away.

It all ended when, in her cap and gown, she was about to walk across the stage. Two university police officers pulled her from the procession line, cuffed her and took her to jail. Kane had filed a stalking and vandalism charge against her. She knew Kane had planned it out that way to humiliate her once again. As she was being led away, he stood smiling. She gave him the one finger salute just before he crossed the stage.

Erin had been placed on probation and mandated to counseling and anger management classes. She completed her probation and master's degree at the same time. Afterwards, she bid farewell to Miami, but not before sending Kane's wife details of her own four year relationship with him. She even included pictures, which she had tons of, showing them at various times during their relationship. She could only imagine his wife's hurt, but it was pain that she knew all too well.

And now here she was being stalked, just as she had been the stalker all those years ago. She wondered if Kane had possibly tracked her down. Maybe he wanted to seek his own revenge.

Erin made it to her front door. She jammed the key in the lock. Just as she was about to open the door, a hand grabbed her shoulder. Erin screamed. It sounded like a siren going off to warn that the tornado was coming. Uncontrollable laughter was what she heard next. Amy took off her hood.

"Goddammit Amy, what the hell!" Erin yelled; she didn't see a damn thing that was funny.

"Oh my god, you should have seen your face," Amy continued in her fit of laughter.

"What the fuck do you want," Erin yelled.

Amy was thrown off. She didn't understand what had made Erin so upset. She had no idea Erin would react this way to a little joke. Erin couldn't believe she had let her guard down. She usually never went anywhere without her mace in her hand and her .22 caliber pistol in her car.

Amy just stared.

"Again, what do you want," Erin exploded.

Amy stuttered. "I was just trying to give you an update on our case we are working on."

"What freaking case," Erin was clueless.

"Mocha and Billy," Amy answered–*duh*, she thought.

Erin looked at her with disgust. She couldn't believe that she had involved herself with such a clown. At the time, it seemed like a good idea to befriend Mocha's secretary.

"Look," Erin began, "I am no longer interested in Billy, so there is no need for us to see each other anymore. I have moved on."

It was Amy's turn to look at Erin like she had just grown horns from her head.

"No, you look. I am not dropping this. I have been working hard getting some good information for you. You can't back out now," Amy stated. "Just wait until you hear what I walked in on"

"I don't care," Erin raised her voice, "whatever you heard or saw, keep it to yourself or don't keep it to yourself. Just leave me out of it." Erin walked into her apartment. She grabbed the door in attempt to slam it in Amy's face, but Amy was a little too quick for her. Amy leaned her shoulder into the door and pushed. Erin stumbled back almost losing her balance.

"What the hell is wrong with you?" Erin screamed?.

"You stupid ass bitch," Amy countered. "You think you're better than me because you have a little more money than I do. Because you went to college, got a degree, you think you can treat people like shit. Well guess what, I have a fucking degree too. You snobbish little bitch. You want to toy with peoples' emotions just for the hell of it. But you picked the wrong motherfucker to mess with this time. Everybody at Baldwin might be scared of you, but I am not."

Erin was terrified. She felt all the emotions of the past rush back to her, only they were compounded this time. She was starring her crazy nightmare right in the face.

"Sit your ass down," Amy demanded.

Erin sat. She looked around her apartment wondering what she could use to hit Amy with. Erin had heard the rumors at work that Amy was not operating with a full deck. Up until now, she thought they were just office rumors. Now she wished she had paid closer attention.

"You have been avoiding me all week," Amy ranted.

"I know you told your secretary to tell me you weren't in each time I called. And then you try to avoid me by working over in the south tower. You know I can't leave my desk to come way over there. Mocha would have a fit if she couldn't find me and needed something. Oh, by the way. How was you walk? You were so busy trying to rush to meet Charles that you didn't realize that I had let out all the air in your fucking tire," Amy laughed.

"Amy, I am sure we can work out what ever issues you are having," Erin said.

"Issues? You're the one who came to me for help. These are your issues. I'm just going to help you get that bitch Mocha out of the way so you can be with Billy," Amy declared. "And I am glad you came to me too. I can't stand Mocha's ass. She thinks she's better than us, you know? I can't wait for you to set her straight and take Billy from her."

"I don't want Billy," Erin purported. She tried to think of something to say to calm Amy down. Amy was proving the rumors to be right. She was some kind of psycho.

"Sure you want Billy. He is handsome, nice, and filthy rich. You just think you can't have him, but when I remove Mocha from the situation, Billy will be all yours."

Amy looked over at Erin.

"Geez, don't look so sad. Auntie Amy is here to help. And once Mocha is gone, you can also be the new HNIC," Amy fell over with laughter once again, "you could never be the HNIC."

Erin didn't catch Amy's joke. She was too busy trying to think of a way to get Amy to leave.

"Get, get it?" Amy asked, "Head Nigga in Charge. You could be the Head Caucasian Woman in Charge. And I'll be your secretary."

Erin knew she had to either get Amy out of her apartment or get herself out of there before this woman truly snapped.

"Now," Amy said with a sinister smile plastered across her face. "Mocha came in early one morning. I pretended not to see her come in. Next thing you know, Billy walks into her office. I thought it was weird that they both came into her office early, so I figured something must be up. Guess what I did?" she asked Erin,. not waiting for her to answer."

"I burst right through the door without knocking. You should have seen the looks on their faces. It was priceless. I made up some bogus shit about needing her signature on some papers and not knowing she had come in early to work. Ha!" Amy laughed, "they were smack dab in the middle of kissing and fondling each other. Ewe," Amy added, "you were right; Mocha is definitely trying to steal your man."

"Amy, Billy is not my man," Erin interjected.

"Not yet he isn't, but just give me a little time and I am going to deliver him to your door step, literally," she added.

Erin tried to get up to make a fast break for the door. Amy was quicker than she looked. With the slight move to her right she stuck her foot out causing Erin to hit the floor with a loud thud. On her way down to the floor, Erin's head caught the corner of the coffee table. The blow to the head caused her to lose consciousness.

MOCHA

*M*ocha was so excited. She could barely make it through the day. Friday had taken its sweet time coming. Although her body had been present at work, her entire thoughts were consumed with Billy and their theater date.

Mocha had finally allowed herself to relax and simply enjoy Billy's company. She thought there was no better way to start a relationship than going to the theater. For as long as she could remember, she could lose herself in a good theatrical production.

The only sour note this week had been Amy. She still couldn't figure out what was going on with her. First, the whole walking into Mocha's office without knocking, then the constant leaving her desk and hanging up the phone every time Mocha had gotten near her desk had caused Mocha to wonder what was up with her.

"Everything shows itself in due time," Mocha had stated.

When her day was finally over, Mocha had rushed home to allow herself plenty of time to get ready for Billy. She had picked out the perfect dress yesterday. It was classy, but showed just enough skin to drive Billy wild. Mocha had always loved the burnt orange color against her milk chocolate skin. She'd picked out a dress with low V-cut back that dipped just above her ass. The front also had a deep Vneck. The split in the front stopped slightly lower than her upper thigh. For once, she was glad that she let her sister talk her into splurging on the burnt orange Roberto Cavalli platform sandals. It would surely drive Billy insane.

Mocha soaked in a hot bath with lemon-scented bath salts. She burned warm vanilla-scented oils. It was just what she needed to release the extra tension from her body after a long week. Mocha had a bad habit of falling asleep in water. True to her nature, she had done just that once again. She was jolted from her sleep by the knocking on her door. She immediately looked at the clock and realized that it had to be Billy at her door. It was 6:00pm. The production started at 7:00pm. She leapt from the tub, quickly grabbed a towel, and rushed to the door.

"Hey Billy," she said, swinging the door open, "I'm sorry, I fell asleep in the tub. How long have you been knocking?" Billy was speechless. He was, again, mesmerized by Mocha's body. She was standing there dripping wet. The things he wanted to do to her body had him speechless. Mocha knew the effect her body could have on men, especially Billy. She reached out, grabbed his arm, and pulled him into her apartment.

The gesture brought him back to himself. He felt his body begin to respond to the sight of Mocha's body. He reached over to take the towel from her that was doing a poor job of concealing her physical attributes. Mocha stood and let him admire her in all her birthday glory. Mocha didn't know if her nipples hardened from the breeze of the air conditioning or from the desire she saw in Billy's eyes. Either way, she was enjoying the way their bodies responded to each other.

Billy closed the distance between them. He used the towel to dry Mocha's wet frame. For the second time, Mocha was enjoying his smooth hands as they explored her body. Billy slowly let the towel drop from his hands, yet continued to caress Mocha's softness. Billy's warm hands sent chills down her spine. His hands encircled her plump ass. He gently lifted mocha to his hips. She swiftly wrapped her legs around his waist. Lowering his head, he did what he'd wanted for months now. He slowly slid his tongue around her erect nipple; that motion with the slight flick of his tongue across the top caused Mocha to moan in pleasure. She allowed her head to fall backwards as she arched her back to give him full access to her breasts. Mocha placed her arms around his neck as Billy positioned her against the wall. He took both of his hands and gently squeezed her breasts as he began sucking her nipples, alternating between the two. It had been years since Mocha let any man touch her this way. At this moment, she felt that it was well worth the wait. Mocha felt herself moving towards her climax.

"Billy," she breathed, "Oh my, that feels so good," she exhaled.

Billy grabbed her waist, lifting her vagina up to his face. Mocha placed her legs on his shoulders, using the wall to balance herself. Billy lightly slid his tongue across her clit. He wanted to taste her as she climaxed. Mocha let out a primitive moan that she knew her neighbors must have heard, but she didn't care. Billy had her body feeling things she had never felt before. Billy slid his tongue in and out of her wetness, causing her to cum in his mouth repeatedly. Mocha was beyond spent. She stopped counting the number of times Billy made her cum after the third time.

"I want to be inside of you," Billy breathed. "Can I make love to you?" he asked.

"Yes, Mocha answered quickly.

Billy carried her to the bedroom. He gently laid her down on the bed. She watched as he undressed. Mocha was excited. She couldn't wait to feel him slid into her. Anxiously, she waited for him to remove his boxers. He hoped she wouldn't be disappointed with his size. Although it didn't really matter at this point–she wanted him regardless of his size. Mocha gasped when he finally released his manhood from confinement. She was grateful that the stereotype wasn't true in Billy's case. He was packing enough size to make her scream out in joy. Making it to the theater wasn't on either of their minds.

Billy was on cloud nine. He couldn't believe that the woman of his dreams actually wanted him. He connected with Mocha on every level. Their lovemaking had been over the moon. She was everything he wanted in a wife. The second they had finished pleasing each other, he began mapping out in his mind how he was going to propose to Mocha. He wanted it to be the proposal that she dreamt about as a little girl.

Mocha was still sound asleep. Billy had been up for the last thirty minutes, fumbling his way around the kitchen. There wasn't much for him to pull together, but he was determined to wake her up to a beautiful breakfast. He found two eggs to scramble, frozen turkey bacon, bread to toast, and coffee. He made a mental note to have his assistant pick up some groceries for Mocha's place. He loved the sound of that. It would actually make a good name for some type of business.

Billy found a tray to place the food. He wished he had a rose to put on the tray, but his impromptu stay last night left him unprepared to treat her like the queen that she was this morning. When she answered the door dripping wet, he could hardly contain himself. He was going to be sure to get tickets to the next production. It was unfortunate that they had to miss the show, but he wouldn't trade a minute of last night for anything. He wanted to spend every moment of every day that he could with Mocha.

12

CHARLES

*C*harles, like his friend, was also on cloud nine the morning after his date with Erin. Although he ended the night early, he was more than excited about the prospect of a relationship developing with Erin.

At the office, Erin put on a front of being an independent, no nonsense bitch, but last night he saw glimpses of a woman who was tired of putting on a facade. She was almost to the point of dropping her guard. Charles knew that she was ready to give herself to him. He wanted her in a bad way, but he was tired of the one night stands. If he allowed her to give herself to him so quickly, he knew that he would lose interest. He was determined to make this one last forever.

Last night, he called Erin to ensure she made it home. He ended up leaving her a message. When she didn't return his call as he requested, he called the driver who confirmed that he dropped her off. Charles decided to call her early to let her know, again, that he enjoyed her company; he also wanted to see if she would like to spend the day at the park. He usually spent his Saturday mornings running five miles through the park. He figured they could have a quick run and maybe enjoy a picnic. When he dialed Erin's number, it went directly to voicemail. He left a message inviting her to the park. He left the address and time for her, asking her to call him back.

Charles couldn't contain his excitement. He moved about his kitchen preparing lunch for the picnic. He whipped up an Italian pasta salad. He mixed in apples, raisins, walnuts and doused it with walnut oil dressing to make a simple fruit salad. Cheese and carrot sticks with hummus rounded out the meal. He grabbed several bottles of water and tossed them into the picnic basket.

Charles waited for two hours to hear from Erin. He was starting to wonder if his inclination had been wrong. Maybe she wasn't interested. It jolted him into to a funk, but he thought perhaps she was just going to meet him at the park. He grabbed his running gear and the picnic basket to head out to the park.

13

ERIN

*E*rin opened her eyes. Her head hurt like hell. She looked around. Her sight was blurry, but she could make out the setting. She was in her room. She didn't remember drinking too much last night at the restaurant with Charles. She tried to move her hand to her head.

"What the fuck!" she exclaimed." Her hands were tied to the bed. Amy walked into the room.

"Oh sweet Erin, you're awake. I made you breakfast. When was the last time you had breakfast in bed? I'm betting it's been a long time. I know you haven't had a man since you moved to town." Amy sat the tray on the bed.

"Let me help you sit up." Erin allowed Amy to help her slide into an upright position. What other choice did she have?

Erin looked down at her clothes. She wondered how she had gotten into her pajamas. Everything from the previous night started to come back to her. She remembered running for the front door. She remembered Amy tripping her, and she remembered hitting her head on the coffee table as she tumbled to the ground. A lone tear rolled down her cheek as she realized the severity of her situation.

"Oh don't cry, Erin. It's ok. I am going to take care of Mocha for you. And guess what? We are going to be best friends forever. You'll marry Billy. And I am going to marry Charles. It just hit me last night. Charles is so sweet and kind. He is really the only person at Baldwin that talks to me, so when he called last night to check to see if you made it in, I thought that was so sweet of him. Then it dawned on me– since you are in love with Billy, and we are like best friends, I should date Billy's best friend, Charles. We could have a double wedding." Amy continued to babble. Erin wondered how she could get herself out of this mess.

"Oh look, we have a voice message," Amy cheerfully stated.

The blinking light on Erin's phone alerted her to a waiting message. Amy picked up the phone from the dresser. She pushed the button. Erin silently cursed herself for not putting a passcode on her cell phone. Amy put the call on speaker.

"Oh, it's my Charles," Amy gushed. They listened as Charles talked about having a great time last night. Amy smiled when he gave the invitation for a picnic in the park.

"What am I going to wear?" Amy asked.

"You are not going to meet Charles," Erin scowled. "Untie me you psycho bitch."

"That's not a very nice thing to say," Amy uttered.

"And barging your way into my apartment, knocking me out, and tying me up are considered nice?" Erin scowled.

"Well, if you weren't trying to kick me out, I wouldn't have had to do those things. You brought that on yourself," Amy accused,"but it's all going to work out in the end, you'll see."

Amy walked over to Erin's closet; she started looking through her clothes.

"What are you doing?" Erin questioned.

"I'm looking for something to wear to meet my future husband, silly. I can't go on a picnic with yesterday's clothes on, now can I?"

"Amy, get out my closet and fucking untie me right now or I swear I am going to call the police on you!" Erin screamed, "you are going to go to jail!"

"But we're friends. Friends don't let friends go to jail. I am going to have to keep you quiet until you calm down." Amy grabbed the duct tape she used to tie Erin to the bed. She tore a strip off and covered Erin's mouth.

"There, that should do. I'll tell you all about the picnic when I get back–toodles,

she sang as she air kissed Erin on both her cheeks. Amy picked up her keys and walked out the door.

"Erin you are stronger than this, don't you dare start crying," Erin told herself, "you didn't beat all that shit in Miami to be taken out by a delusional secretary."

Erin tried wriggling her hands free. It wasn't working. As much as she pulled, the tape didn't give way. A lone tear streamed down her face followed by several more. Within minutes, she was crying uncontrollably.

CHARLES

*C*harles constantly watched his phone. He was hoping he would hear from Erin on the way to the park. 20 minutes later and still no word. Charles glanced in the back seat at the picnic basket.

"Guess that will go to waste," he said aloud.

Charles got out of the car and began stretching his legs. He was just about to set on his run when he heard someone calling his name.

"Charles, hey I thought that was you," Amy breathed. How long have you been running here?

"Amy?" Charles questioned, unsure if he had gotten her name correct.

"You remembered," Amy smiled.

"I run here every Saturday," he answered.

"Oh, well that explains why I've never seen you here before. I usually run on Sundays," Amy lied, "but it was such a beautiful day; I thought I would get an extra run in this weekend."

Amy leaned over to look into the backseat of Charles car.

"You're having a picnic. Are you meeting someone here?" She asked.

"I was supposed to, but it looks like she's not going to make it," he answered.

Amy smiled, "Maybe I can join you. No need to let all that good food got to waste."

Charles thought it was a little weird that Amy would invite herself to his picnic, but he was too much of a gentleman to turn her down.

"Sure," he replied. But let's get this run in first.

"Ok," Amy replied.

Charles didn't know what her deal was, but for sure, he knew she was no runner. A minute into the run she started to lag behind and he wasn't even close to running his usual speed. He didn't know much about Amy. She stopped by the bistro at least twice a day. It was once in the morning to pick her and Mocha's latte up, and again during lunch to have the cranberry tuna salad sandwich with a side of fruit salad.

Occasionally, Charles would add a cookie to her order as a way of thanking her, but he did that for all of his regular customers. Amy, however, had taken it to mean more than it was worth. She thought that she was the only one who received these extra treats. For sure, she thought Charles wanted her–and she wanted him.

Charles decided to cut the run short. He told Amy he wasn't really feeling the run and asked if she wanted to just walk back to the car to get the picnic basket.

"*Praise Jesus*," Amy thought to herself. "Well if you're sure you don't want to keep going…"

"No, I think I've had enough," Charles feigned disinterest.

It was quick walk back to the car to retrieve the basket. If Charles had to guess, they'd only run about a mile. They small talked on the way back, mostly about the weather. Charles really didn't see much that they would have in common, but since he didn't have anything else to do and hadn't heard back from Erin, he figured Amy's company was better than no company at all.

Charles spread out a blanket on the grass. Amy happily plopped down. She eagerly removed the food from the basket. She was very complimentary of all the food that Charles prepared.

"The person you were expecting is really going to miss out on this wonderful meal you prepared. I just love your food at the bistro," Amy declared.

Charles smiled. He loved to receive compliments on his craft. He absolutely loved being a chef. It was the best year of his life learning to become a chef after completing graduate school. No one understood why, after earning an MBA and being rich, he wanted to go take classes to learn to be a chef.

He had only ever told his friend Billy the truth. His mother's life-long dream had been to become a chef. She was so busy with being a wife and mother that she never had the chance to seriously pursue her dream. What little free time she had left after ensuring that her family had what they needed, she spent perfecting recipes on dishes she would serve to her family and friends. Charles had loved spending time in the kitchen with his mother. She taught him how to cook, bake, and create master pieces with the simplest of ingredients. It was those same recipes that he used in the bistro.

Amy's compliments reminded him of his mother. It didn't matter if he bombed a recipe or not, she was 100% supportive.

"Thanks," Charles responded.

Charles found himself opening up, talking to Amy about his hopes and desires for the future. He talked about one day marrying and having kids. Amy, with her warped thinking, took it to mean that he wanted to marry her and have kids. She couldn't wait to tell Erin the good news. She knew Erin would be excited. They were both a step closer to getting the men of their dreams.

Charles walked Amy to her car and thanked her for her company. She thanked him as well.

"I guess we will see each other on Monday at work," Amy stated.

"I'm guessing we will," Charles replied.

Charles couldn't wait to get Amy on her way. Although Amy was good company, he had wanted to check his phone to see if Erin had at least returned his call. He was disappointed when he looked at his phone. He had no missed calls and no text messages.

Charles started to assume that maybe Erin wasn't interested in him. He wondered if he could have picked up the wrong vibe from her at the dinner last night. Or perhaps she was ticked off at him for ending their evening early.

Charles didn't know what his next move should be. He sat in the car thinking. He decided to call his friend to see if he had any much needed advice for him. Billy answered after the third ring.

"How did it go last night?" Billy answered the phone without a greeting.

"I don't know," Charles stated.

"What do you mean you don't know?" Billy questioned.

"I thought it went well, but I have been trying to call her all day and she hasn't responded," Charles answered.

"Did you follow the plan?" Billy asked.

"Step by step," Charles said.

"Do you think she's playing hard to get?" Billy asked.

"I hope not, I don't have time for bullshit," Charles said. "What should I do?"

"Nothing," Billy answered, "you don't want to start to seem desperate. You have done your part, now just wait on her to make the next move.

"Are you sure?" Charles worried.

"Positive," Billy added.

MOCHA

*M*ocha and Billy spent the rest of the weekend together. After breakfast, they continued to enjoy each other sexually. Each explored the other's body and brought sensual pleasure that matched heights neither thought possible. They sexed their way through lunch, but decided to order dinner from Masraff's on Saturday night.

"I am going to have to do a three hour workout tomorrow after eating all of this," Mocha declared.

Billy had ordered garlic seared calamari, mushroom ravioli, scallops, and seafood paella. He rounded out the meal with Texas peach crème brulee. Mocha was in heaven. She loved to eat diverse food, which is why she had to ensure that she carved out time during her day to do cardio exercises–otherwise, she would be as big as a house.

Billy was such a gentlemen. He was extremely attentive and catered to Mocha's every need. He literally would not let her lift a finger. He would ask her what she would like to taste, then proceed with feeding her. After each bite, he gingerly wiped her mouth. He'd claimed he wanted to treat her like the queen that she was born to be. Mocha melted when hearing his declaration. She didn't think she could resist falling in love with him, even if she wanted to, but clearly she wanted him as much as he wanted her.

Mocha and Billy finished the last bite of crème brulee together as he licked the crumbs from her mouth. He encircled her lips with his tongue before sliding it into her mouth. Mocha happily accepted the sweetness of it between her lips. They had christened just about every piece of furniture throughout her small space. The kitchen counter had seen way more than it should have. The coffee table proved to be made of the strongest wood as it held the weight of their bodies suspended in air. The couch, dining table, shower, and wash room all took peeks as the couple tenderly expressed their love.

By Sunday morning, Billy had everything he needed to fix a proper meal for Mocha. His assistant had gone grocery shopping just as he had requested. Billy met her downstairs to retrieve the items he had listed for her to purchase. He had exactly what he needed to end their weekend with a tantalizing meal that would surely continue to upgrade his status in Mocha's eyes. Billy was proud of his culinary skills. Charles had taught him a thing or two about whipping up quick, but tasteful meals that would impress any woman. His best dish just so happened to be breakfast enchiladas.

First he cooked the sausage, stirring it until it crumbled. Then he drained it, added butter, green onions, cilantro, and sautéed it for a few minutes. Next, he added salt, pepper, and eggs to the mixture. He allowed the eggs to thicken before removing them from the heat. After adding cheese, he folded the mixture into tortillas. He poured cheese sauce over the top and sprinkled the dish with a mixture of halved grape tomatoes, sliced green onions, and chopped fresh cilantro.

Billy hadn't allowed Mocha to step one foot into the kitchen, although she tried on several occasions. He would quickly turn her back around to finish scanning the documents she'd brought home from the office to complete.

As Mocha placed the first bite of enchiladas into her mouth, she moaned outward with pleasure. It was the best thing she had tasted all weekend.

"Billy Baldwin, I do believe you are trying to make me fall in love with you," she joked.

"That I am," Billy responded.

Mocha smiled at him from across the table. Billy smiled back at her. They both loved the feeling of falling in love. Mocha stood, seductively walking over to Billy. She wanted to please him as much as he had been pleasing her. Mocha bent over, placing her soft lips against Billy's. The tenderness shown each to the other was what Mocha had been dreaming about since her teen years.

Mocha slid down between his legs. She opened his robe, allowing his manhood to hang freely. She admired what she saw, still unable to believe that he had such a massive penis. Mocha used her tongue to encircle the tip. This time it was Billy who allowed moans to escape his lips. When Mocha finally slid her lips down his shaft, she pressed her tongue down the length, causing Billy's body to quiver. Mocha was so into pleasing Billy that each time he moaned, she would take him deeper into her mouth. She swore she felt his penis kissing the back of her throat, yet he was only in halfway. She used her hand to work the remaining inches.

"I want to taste you," Billy exhaled.

"I want and need to please you," Mocha said unintelligibly due to his massive dick in her mouth."

Billy tried to pull her to him but Mocha had her lips locked around him. She sped up her motion, sending him into overdrive. Billy was definitely about to explode. Mocha anxiously waited. She wanted his protein in her mouth. Seconds later, she was slurping the remnants and loving the taste of his semen.

Billy was spent. He didn't think he could want her more than he already did, but having her lips wrapped around his dick had increased his desire tenfold. He grabbed Mocha's body, lifting her to a straddling position on his lap. Mocha eased down on his erection. Mocha was shocked that he still had one. Mandingo is the one word that came to her mind, although he had probably no clue that there was even such a thing as the Mandinka people. Hours later, the two lay in bed wrapped in each other's arms.

"Mocha," Billy stuttered, "I really want to get to know you better." What he really wanted to say was that he had already fallen in love with her, but he couldn't decide if it was the right time or not.

"I am enjoying your company," Mocha responded, "I want to get to know you better too." Mocha raised up to plant a kiss on his lips.

"I hate to have to do this, but I really need to go into the office. I didn't get through half the paperwork that I was supposed to finish. I also have to write out my Monday Morning Message." Mocha had been doing a Monday Morning Message for the last 2 years, where she addressed the employees at Baldwin. Each employee was required to stop and watch the message live on one of the big screen monitors located throughout the building.

"I'll drive you," Billy volunteered. At this point, he would follow Mocha to Timbuktu and back if it meant he could be next to her.

"Ok," Mocha gleamed.

After showering and getting dressed, Billy drove Mocha over to Baldwin Towers. On the drive over, Billy decided to pop his slow jams' disc into the player. Mocha slid closer to Billy and laid her head on his shoulder as she listened to the sound of Anthony Hamilton caressing her as he sang *"The Point of It All."*

Billy began singing along with Anthony. To Mocha's surprise, not only did he know the words, but actually sounded good. Billy couldn't believe how great things had gone for he and Mocha this weekend. Billy's mind started to drift to how he would ask Mocha to marry him. It had to be huge. He contemplated flying her to Dallas to have dinner at The Wolfgang Puck at Reunion Tower. He felt like he was on top of the world, so what better place to ask her to become his wife than 561 feet in the air. Billy was getting excited about the possibilities. He could have a plane fly around the tower with a banner asking her to marry him.

Mocha had dozed off on the drive over. By the time she awoke, they were pulling into the garage at Baldwin. Billy kissed her head. He loved the innocent dazed look she had on her face. She looked around to see where they had gone.

"We made it," Billy stated.

Mocha stretched as Billy parked, got out the car, and walked to the other side. He opened the door for Mocha, holding out his hand to help her from the car. She placed her hand in his, instantly feeling the warmth that traveled throughout his body. Hand in hand, they walked through the doors at Baldwin.

Mocha wasn't sure anybody else would be at work today. Briefly, she thought about removing her hand from his. She contemplated letting others know that they were dating, but decided that if Billy didn't care, neither should she.

Billy walked Mocha to her office before leaving to head to his own office. He figured that maybe he should get a little work done as well. Before leaving, he lightly kissed Mocha on her temple. She blushed.

Mocha was able to get all of her work done in a short amount of time. It didn't surprise her, because she loved her position at Baldwin. Mocha began feeling a little adventurous. She decided to take advantage of the building being empty. She stood and quickly removed all of her clothing leaving only her matching lace bra and panty set. After undressing, she called Billy and told him she was ready. When he knocked on the door, Mocha breathed the words *come in*. Billy walked in to a pleasant surprise.

"My, my, my," he stated.

Mocha was sitting atop her desk with her legs gaped as if she was waiting for Billy to take his rightful place.

16

ERIN

*E*rin finally pulled her emotions together. After getting out that much needed cry, she tried to come up with a plan. Clearly, Amy was suffering from low self-esteem. She had a wounded heart, much like what Erin had when she decided to leave Miami. Hope for the future was Erin's saving grace. She had to somehow convince Amy that she was on her side. She needed to build up her self-esteem. She had to give her hope.

Amy was the happiest she had been in a long time after the picnic with Charles. She bounced into the room where Amy was being held. She sat down on the bed, swinging her feet in the air as she let out a girlish squeal.

"I had the best time today with Charles. I totally picked the right guy," Amy gushed.

Erin started to mumble. She knew Amy wouldn't be able to understand a word she was saying. It was her way to get the duct tape off of her mouth. She needed to put her own plan into motion. Just as she expected Amy ripped the tape from Erin's mouth. Erin howled out in pain. Amy laughed, saying "sorry."

The first word that popped into Erin's mind was *"Bitch,"* but she held her tongue saying, "It's no big deal, bestie."

"Oh I like that, we are best friends forever," Amy agreed.

"So tell me what happened with Charles," Erin stated.

Erin listened as Amy rambled on about the run and picnic with Charles. Erin bit her tongue to keep from saying anything that would result in Amy covering her mouth back up with tape.

When she finished with all the details, Erin responded. "I am so happy for you! You really deserve this and so much more."

"And guess what?" Amy said.

"What," Erin asked?

"We are going to make sure you get the man of your dreams too," Amy beamed.

Amy filled Erin in on her plan to get Mocha away from Billy. All Erin could do was listen. Amy told of how she had placed a hidden camera in Mocha's office.

"I think I would make a really good private investigator," Amy blurted.

Amy's facial expression took on a sinister look. Erin was afraid for not only herself, but also for Charles, Billy, and Mocha. What started out as simple fact finding mission had somehow turned into a different version of Silence of the Lambs!

"That bitch really thinks she is better than us, but I've got something really juicy planned for Mocha," Amy rambled, "who the fuck names their kid Mocha any damned way? Just because she is black doesn't mean she has to be named after something stupid like coffee. Hell, my mom didn't name me milk and I am as white as they come."

"This woman is truly psychotic," Erin thought. *"She is sitting here rambling about a name. Who does that?"*

"Amy," Erin called. She had to say her name several times to snap her out of her trance.

"What!" Amy yelled.

"I was just wondering if I could use the restroom," Erin stammered.

"Silly, of course you can," Amy sang. "You don't have to ask to go to the bathroom."

Amy cut the remaining duct tape that was holding Erin strapped in place.

Erin thought to herself that this was her chance. She needed to make a break for the door. It was now or never. She slowly moved to the edge of the bed. She stood on wobbly legs. She was as frightened as she had ever been in her entire life, but she knew that it was going to take courage to get out of this situation. Erin walked towards the bathroom. Although it was in her room, it was closer to the bedroom door. She used her peripheral vision to check Amy's positioning. When she felt she was close enough to the door, she broke out into a full sprint. Amy leapt to her feet and charged after Erin. Erin made it to the front door. She placed her hand on the knob when she felt the force of a freight train slam her body into the door. Her head ricocheted off the door frame, causing her to lose consciousness once again.

Amy was livid. "You were supposed to be my friend Erin!" she yelled. "You can't leave me!"

She watched as Erin lie in a puddle of blood that was oozing from her head. Amy checked her pulse. She needed to ensure that Erin was still breathing. Tying Erin back up hadn't been in her plan, but she would do what was necessary until Erin decided to go along with her plan.

She reached down to grab Erin's arms. She drug her limp body back into the bedroom. Once there, she tugged and pushed to get Erin completely back into the bed. She tied Erin's arms back to the bed post. She went to the bathroom to get a towel. She soaked it in alcohol, and used it to clean the gash on Erin's forehead. Erin winced in pain. The agony she felt throughout her body was excruciating.

Amy talked to Erin periodically as she cleaned her wound. The last thing Erin heard was Amy telling her not to worry, that she would be back tomorrow to bring her something to eat. She had to go check on her cats. She air kissed Erin saying "toodles" on the way out of the front door.

17

CHARLES

*C*harles was beginning to think that his dinner date with Erin had been a fluke. She hadn't returned any of his calls. When his phone finally did ring, it was a delivery service making arrangements to have a few things dropped off for the bistro.

Charles was disappointed. He was beginning to wonder if something had happened to Erin. The driver had confirmed that she made it home, but not returning his previous calls was bordering on rude behavior. He thought back to the look in her eyes at the restaurant. There was no way he could have misconstrued the desire in her eyes. She was definitely feeling him and he knew it.

"So what's the problem," he said aloud. Charles decided to drive by Erin's place to see if she was ok. Afterwards, he would drop by the bistro to receive the shipment.

Charles pulled into the parking lot at Erin's condo. He easily spotted her candy apple red BMW. He assumed she had the tire repaired and dropped off to her. Charles backed his car into a parking space on the other side of the lot. He didn't want to seem like a prowler or for her to see him lurking outside her place.

As soon as he turned the car off, he was surprised to see Amy coming out the front door of Erin's condo. He never figured her to be a person that Erin would hang out with. Amy was as odd as they came. He thought back to how she invited herself to his picnic. He didn't want to be rude, so he had allowed her to join him. He figured there was no sense in wasting the food he had prepared for Erin.

Charles closely watched Amy. Her behavior was curious. She looked around from side to side as if she was trying to avoid someone or something. Charles frowned at her nonverbal cues. She got into her car still checking her surroundings. Charles slid down in his seat to keep from being recognized.

"What the heck is going on," he chided.

Charles decided to dial Erin's number once again. It rang several times before rolling over to voicemail.

"Hey Erin, it's Charles. I'm really starting to worry about you. I was thinking you really enjoyed our date. I sure did. Give me a call back to let me know you are ok," Charles babbled. Once he disconnected the call, he stated, "where are you Erin?" Charles had a bad feeling about this. His gut feelings were never wrong. He decided to dial the driver again who dropped Erin at home after their date.

"Hey Dan, this is Charles. When you dropped Erin off the other night, are you sure she made it into her condo before you pulled off?" There was a brief silence on the other end. Charles assumed that he was thinking back to the night before answering.

"Now that you mention it, she said she was going to check her mail. I asked her if she wanted me to wait for her, but she insisted that she would be fine. I watched as she walked over to the mailboxes before she shooed me away. Is she ok," Dan asked?

"I'm not sure," Charles responded, "I haven't been able to reach her, but that's not abnormal. It was our first dat,e so I can't say that I definitely should have heard from her by now, but my senses are a little off. I'm hoping she has just been busy and hasn't had the time to call me back just yet."

"Ok, well let me know if you need me to do anything," Dan requested.

"Thanks Dan, I will."

Charles felt no better after the call than before he made it. In fact, he felt worse not knowing if Erin actually made it inside after retrieving her mail. He cursed himself for not dropping her off personally.

Charles was getting antsy. He opened the door to his car and walked over to Erin's front door. He leaned over placing his ear against the door. He felt awkward doing this but was desperate for answers.

Charles almost jumped out of his skin when the door across the walkway opened.

"What are you doing mister?" a little boy asked.

"I'm trying to check on my friend," Charles answered.

"It looked like you were eavesdropping to me," the little boy stated. Charles ignored his statement.

"Have you seen the lady that lives here?" Charles questioned.

"You mean Erin?" he asked.

"Yes, have you seen Erin?"

"No, just some weird looking chick. She's been coming and going from here all weekend. I tried to talk to her, but she just ignored me," he admitted.

Charles knew he had to be referring to Amy. He decided to knock on Erin's door. He held his breath waiting to see if she answered. If, in fact, she was ok, he would look like a stalker and could possibly sink any chance that he might have at a relationship with her. He and the little boy waited.

Charles knocked again. Erin could hear someone knocking at her door. She tried her best to make some noise. She needed to alert the person knocking that she needed some help. She moaned as loud as she could. She knew it was probably impossible for them to hear her with her mouth being taped up.

"Hey," Charles said as he turned to the little boy. "Can you give me a call when you see Erin or if the other lady comes back to the apartment? It doesn't matter the day or time."

"How much?" the little boy asked.

"How much what?" Charles responded.

"How much are you going to pay me for spying on Erin?" Charles chuckled. He was being shaken down by a half-pint.

"$20 bucks," Charles answered.

The little boy's face lit up.

Charles reached into his wallet and pulled out a $20 bill. He handed it to him along with a piece of paper with his name and number scribbled on it.

"Thanks, Mr. Charles," he gleamed.

"You're welcome, Charles retorted. "Remember, any time of day or night."

18

AMY

*a*my was driving to her house to feed her cats when her cellular phone buzzed. A giddy Amy looked at the phone twice to ensure she was seeing the message correctly. She had questioned spending such an enormous amount of money for the video camera with motion detector that would also alert her to when it had been activated.

"Mocha didn't tell me she was going into the office today. What's this little impromptu visit to the office all about?" Amy inquired She sped up. She wanted to get home to pull the video feed up on her computer. She hoped it would be something juicy that she could use to cause severe damage to Mocha and her career.

Amy pulled into the driveway, almost on two wheels. She jogged to her front door with adrenaline running through her veins. She walked into her study plopping, down in front of her desktop computer. She quickly entered the password for the computer, and then for the video feed. The video was automatically recording in live time.

"Oh shit Mocha, that feels so damn good," Billy's voice boomed through Amy's speakers.

"Well, well, well," Amy retorted. She sat and watched Billy and Mocha as they redefined for her what astronomical sex looked like.

Watching them go at it had caused Amy to get heated herself. She pulled her shirt up, undid her bra, and began squeezing her own nipples. She longed to feel Charles' hands doing what she had to do to please her.

"Charles, that feels so good," Amy exhaled. Her breathing increased as though she were really enjoying the touch of his hands massaging her nipples. "I want to feel you inside me Charles," Amy said as she reached over to open the drawer next to the computer table. She pulled out her dildo, quickly undressing. She slid the massive fake penis as deep as she could into her folds. Amy moaned in pleasure. She imagined Billy's voice being Charles telling her how good her pussy was. When she looked over at the screen, Billy had Mocha bent over the chaise lounge as he entered her and sexed her from the back. Mocha was enjoying every inch of Billy's length. She was very vocal in telling him how good he was making love to her. Listening to their sex talk caused Amy to move step by step, closer to reaching her orgasm. She was in rhythm with Billy. Every time he would thrust, so would she. Every word that Mocha uttered, she too uttered. Amy, Billy, Mocha, and fake Charles all reached their climax at the same time. They all lay spent, not wanting to move.

Billy was the first to speak. "I love you Mocha." It was met with silence. Amy rose up to look at the monitor. She had a scowl plastered on her face.

"It's ok if you don't feel the same way just yet," Billy stated. "My sole mission from this point on is to make you fall in love with me. I want to…"

"I love you Billy Baldwin," Mocha cut him off. Billy smiled. He pulled Mocha into an embrace, lightly placing soft kisses all over her face. Mocha giggled. Amy seethed.

"I love you too Charles" Amy exclaimed. Amy started placing kisses all over the entire dildo that she held in her hand. She licked the piece up and down.

Just as Billy and Mocha started in on another session of lovemaking, so did Amy with her stand-in Charles. Amy slid it into her mouth. She worked her lips up and down the dildo as if it were Charles himself. "You like that baby?" she asked. Amy was deep throating it and giving it everything she had. Once again, she was about to have an orgasm. She howled out in pleasure. Once she regained her composure she looked over at the screen. It showed Mocha's office empty. She wondered when they had left. She rewound the recording to see Mocha and Billy walking out of the office hand in hand.

Amy smiled. "I have just what I need to bring Miss Mocha down off her high horse. Once everyone sees what a whore she is, she won't have a choice but to resign. Erin will get Mocha's position and Billy Baldwin, and I will get Charles. We can have a double wedding," she surmised.

"Our kids will grow up best friends. We will live in the same neighborhood, just a few houses apart. They'll attend the same schools. If it's a boy and a girl, they can get married and we'll share grandkids." Amy was delusional. Her mood changed like the wind. The sinister look had once again returned to her face.

"And if it doesn't work out like that, I'll have to take all of them out. It will be as easy as taking candy from a baby."

Amy quickly copied the file. She went to check on her cats. After feeding them, she took a quick shower and changed clothes. She picked up her keys and headed out the door. On the entire ride to Baldwin Tower, she daydreamed about seeing the look on Mocha's face when everyone learned the truth about her, especially her boss, William Baldwin Senior. "Hell I might just get a raise out of this myself. I'm sure Mr. Baldwin doesn't want a bitch like Mocha as his daughter-in-law," Amy laughed.

Amy devised her plan as she drove. By the time she reached the office, she had everything mapped out. She spoke to the security guard, telling him she would be in her office working for the next two to three hours. First, she went into Mocha's office to check the hidden camera. It was still in the same position. She knew it would be, but decided to check anyway. The next thing she did was go into the tech room on the eighth floor. Amy was very meticulous in putting things into place. It took her longer than expected, but after two and half hours, she accomplished her mission. All she had to do now was to sit back and wait.

After leaving Baldwin Towers, she stopped by Souper Salad to pick up dinner for herself and Erin. She stuffed one of everything from the buffet in the to-go box to ensure that she would get something that Erin would like. She also added in cheesecake and brownies. It was time for them to celebrate.

Amy pulled into the parking space next to Erin's car. As she was walking towards the door to Erin's apartment. The door to unit across the hall swing open.

"Do you need any help with all that stuff?" a little boy asked.

Amy frowned. She hated little boys. She could play all day little girls, combing their hair and having tea parties, but boys were nasty. She wouldn't dream of letting him put his filthy little hands anywhere near her food.

"No, thank you. I can manage," she barked. The little boy wasn't fazed by her brashness.

"Are you a friend of Erin's?" he asked. Amy rolled her eyes; she was ready to get the food into the house. It was heavy.

"Yes, I am. Now shoo," she waved.

"Well I haven't seen her lately," he continued.

"Look you little," Amy stopped herself before she said too much. The last thing she needed was him snooping around or telling his mother something stupid.

"Erin has been sick and I have been taking care of her. So if you don't mind, I really need to get these things into the house, Amy lied."

"Why didn't you just say so," the little boy said as he bounced back into his front door. Once he closed the door, Amy grumbled, "nosey little fucker."

Amy used Erin's key to open the door. She sat all the food down on the table.

"Honey I'm home, she sang out." She took a tray, two plates, and two glasses from the cupboard. She placed a little of everything on both plates, pouring juice into the glasses. She carried the tray into the bedroom. Erin sat shooting daggers at Amy.

After sitting the tray down, Amy walked over to Erin, ripping the tape from her mouth. Erin yelped out in pain.

"Sorry hun," Amy replied, "but it hurts less if you do it quickly."

"I have to use the bathroom," Erin mumbled.

"Oh snap, I forgot about that one little minor detail," Amy added. Amy ran back to kitchen. Erin could hear her opening and closing doors. She wondered what psycho bullshit she was about to force on her. She didn't know how much more of this she could take. The one thing that was keeping her going was thinking about her possible future with Charles. Amy burst back into the room with a pan in her hand.

"What is that for?" Erin stated.

"For you to use the bathroom," Amy explained.

"Seriously," Erin hissed.

"The last time I let you go to the bathroom, you tried to make a run for it. I don't know if I can trust you just yet, but you'll eventually come around. You all always do," Amy acknowledged.

Erin didn't ask any more questions. She heard Amy loud and clear when she referenced *you all*. Erin knew that meant she probably wasn't the first person that Amy had done this to.

Erin followed Amy's instructions. She had never been so humiliated in all her life.

When Amy told her to roll over so that she could place the pan up under her, she did. It hurt like hell as her thighs and ass pressed down on the cooking pan. She relieved herself. She had no other choice. Erin cringed as Amy wiped between her legs, cleaning her vagina. No other woman had touched her there since her mother had when she was a toddler.

Erin ate her food as she listened to Amy babble on about her plan to humiliate Mocha. Erin wanted no part of this. She initially wanted Mocha out of the way, but that was before she had gotten to know Charles. Everything that had happened so far was a direct result of what she had put into motion. A lone tear streamed down her face.

"Oh Erin, what's wrong?" Amy inquired.

Amy reached over, wiping the tear away. She rubbed Erin's face. "It will all be over soon, just you wait and see."

19

CHARLES

*C*harles had gone to the gym after leaving the bistro. He thought he saw Amy when he was leaving the building, but didn't get a very good look at the woman as the elevator was closing. He surmised that it probably wasn't her. Not many people worked the weekends at Baldwin. The company really stressed employees taking time for themselves and their families. It was one reason so many people wanted to land a job there.

Charles had spent the last three hours pushing himself to the brink of passing out. He only worked out this hard when he was stressed. He was finishing up his workout by sitting in the whirl pool relaxing. It was his treat to his body for holding up under all the pressure he'd just put it through.

Charles jumped as the ringtone from his cell phone echoed throughout the wet area. He looked down at the phone not recognizing the number. He hoped it would be Erin.

"Hello," he answered.

"Hey mister," a little voice responded. Charles knew right off it was the little boy who lived across the hall from Erin. He pushed himself up from the water sitting on the side of the whirl pool.

"Hey little man," Charles replied, "Do you have some information for me?

"Sure do. That lady came back. I asked her if she was friends with Erin. She said yes. I asked her where was Erin. She said she has been sick."

"Did she say anything else," Charles inquired?

"Nope, but she was just acting weird."

"Yeah, she's kind of weird all the time," Charles stated, "thanks for your help, little man."

"No problem, do you still need me to be on lookout?" he asked?

"Absolutely," Charles replied, "call me if you see or hear anything weird."

Charles was really only toying with the boy. He was satisfied now just knowing that Erin had been sick. He assumed that was the reason she had not returned his calls. He looked forward to seeing her at work in the morning. Charles smiled. He couldn't wait to watch her stroll up to the bistro. Images of her sauntering up to him last week when she was staking her claim invaded his brain. He instantly became aroused. His manhood was now standing at full attention.

Charles reached down between his legs. He couldn't stop himself. He began stroking himself in a slow methodical motion enjoying the sensation pulsating through his body. He imagined Erin walking towards him. With each step she took, she removed a layer of clothing.

By the time she reached him, not a single article of clothing was left covering her body. She quickly placed her hand where his had been. She continued the journey of heightening his arousal by stroking him fast, long, and hard. Before he could reach his climax, she covered his penis with her mouth. Charles laid his head back on the floor as his intensity grew from within. A few minutes more and his semen was spewing into the whirlpool.

Charles looked around the wet area. He had never done anything like this out in public before. He was a little embarrassed and hoped no one had seen him. He made a mental note to have the building custodians to clean the whirlpool before he left the building.

Whatever this was that he was feeling for Erin definitely had him bugging in a way that he wasn't sure was healthy. If anyone had seen what he had just done, his friend Billy would have no choice but to kick him out of Baldwin Towers for sure. He knew he needed to explore a relationship with Erin and he wanted it, but it was hard looking ahead since she had been missing in action.

One thing that cheered Charles up was the fact that he would get a chance to see Erin. Monday morning couldn't come quick enough for him.

After leaving Baldwin, Charles still couldn't shake the feeling that something was off. Never once had he seen Erin and Amy together. In fact, he remembered Amy making disparaging remarks about Erin. So now, in the blink of an eye, they were as thick as thieves. It just didn't add up. As he was about to exit the freeway in route to his place, he decided to swing back by Erin's condo to see if Amy's car was still parked out front. As he turned into the parking lot, Amy's car was the first thing he spotted. Charles looked at the clock on his dashboard. It read 9:16 pm. "Why would she still be here," he whispered. Charles pulled into the spot next to Erin's car. He got out, peeping into the windows of her BMW. He didn't know what he was expecting to find, but was compelled to take a look. Nothing seemed out of place. He looked back at the windows of Erin's place. The lights were on in what he assumed was the living area and bedroom.

Charles heard a door close and immediately knelt down. He wasn't sure who was coming out of their condo, but if it was Erin or Amy, he didn't want to be seen lurking about. He lifted his head a bit to give him a better view. It was Amy. She briskly walked to her car. Just as before, she looked around as if she were hiding from someone or hiding something. She closed the door to her car and spun out the parking lot as if she were being chased.

Charles nearly pissed his pants as he was still crouched down beside the car and someone reached out touching his shoulder. He quickly stood and faced the person.

"Goddammit kid, you nearly gave me a heart attack," Charles gasped.

"You're not a very good private investigator," the kid laughed.

"No, I guess I'm not if I just let you walk up behind me and didn't even notice," Charles explained. "What's your name any way?"

"Tommy," he answered.

"Is that short for Thomas," Charles inquired.

"Nope, just Tommy," he answered.

"Well Tommy, why are you outside this late at night?"

"It's not late, it's just 9:00, and I was taking the trash out." He held up the empty can to emphasize his point.

"Besides, I am 10 now. 10 year olds can stay out later than little kids."

"That's right," Charles agreed.

"So Tommy, have you seen Erin at all today?" he asked.

"No, and I have been watching out really well! I haven't seen anybody but that weird lady."

Charles glanced back at Erin's windows. The lights were still on. He thought for a moment. As he began walking, Tommy asked what he was about to do.

"I'm going to knock on Erin's door," Charles spoke.

"I don't think that's what they would say to do in a private investigators class," Tommy warned.

"Probably not," Charles laughed, "but I really need to see if Erin is ok."

Charles and Tommy stood outside of the door as he knocked. They listened intently waiting for her to answer. Charles knocked for what seemed like 10 minutes.

"Dude, I don't think she's in there. If she was, she would have answered by now," Tommy surmised.

"I think you must be right," Charles admitted, "you better get on in the house yourself before your mother starts to worry about you."

"Ok," Tommy answered. "See you tomorrow."

Charles didn't bother asking how he knew he would be there again tomorrow. He just assumed that his intent could be seen scrawled across his face.

MOCHA

*M*ocha had been up since 4:30 am. She was an early riser. She was one of those people who were pumped up about all the possibilities of the day. Ever since she was a little girl, she had loved those military commercials that claimed they got more done before breakfast than most people did all day. That was Mocha to a tee. She was dressed and out the door by 5:30 am. By 6:00 am, she was sitting behind her desk, pouring over her notes for her Monday Morning Message that would be broadcast on every monitor throughout the building. There were a total of 252 monitors in the building. Every floor, break room, office, and elevator had one.

During the message, Mocha would cover the company's weekly losses, gains, acquisitions, goals, and high achievers. She would then announce the employees of the week. It was why most people tuned in. Being named employee of the week came with a $1000.00 bonus. Before Mocha was promoted to the management team, she had set the company record winning for 25 consecutive weeks before Erin came along and broke her streak. Although short lived, she and Erin battled back and forth winning until Mocha wasn't eligible anymore as a supervisor. Mocha looked over at her wall clock. It was time for her to walk down to the communications suite.

Amy was at her desk, pretending to be busy. Mocha knew she was pretending because she hadn't given her any work to do just yet. Mocha wondered what was going on with her. Normally, she would have buzzed Mocha ten times already asking for something to do. Mocha didn't like the vibes that she was getting from Amy lately. This happened quite frequently with Mocha and her secretaries. Initially, they were excited to simply have a job, but after a while, they would start to slack off—that's when Mocha would replace them. She averaged a new secretary just about every two years. She had hoped that Amy would be different. It was the price that she had to pay for being a type A personality. She needed a secretary who had a type A personality, but that was mostly unheard of. Most type A's were so pressed to be successful they never stayed in lower level jobs, so Mocha was forced to have her secretary's transferred to other departments and seek out new ones.

Damn, Mocha thought, *this woman is not even going to speak. Where is the respect?*

"Good morning Amy," Mocha breathed. *No sense in me acting like I wasn't raised right just because she wasn't.*

"Good morning," Amy growled.

Amy was really behaving like she was the boss and Mocha was her employee. Amy was confident that, after today, Mocha would be but a distant memory. She couldn't wait to get back to the condo and tell Erin everything that happened. Today would be the day that they'd start their new lives with Charles and Billy.

Mocha smiled; she wasn't going to pay Amy any attention, because after today, she would be somebody else's headache. She planned to stop by personnel on her way back to her office after the morning message.

Mocha left the office bumping right into Billy.

"What a pleasant surprise," she heard Billy's husky voice. Mocha smiled.

"That it is, Mr. Baldwin."

"Are you on your way to the communications suite for your morning message?" he asked.

She answered "yes," knowing full well that he already knew the answer to his question.

"Well, don't let me keep you beautiful lady." Billy gave the usher pose, mocking a bow. Mocha walked by, giving her sexiest strut for him to lust after. She looked back over her shoulder, winking at him before entering the elevator.

Mocha sat in front of the teleprompter, reciting notes she had uploaded as they appeared on the screen. She could give these messages without the prompter, but chose to have them on in case she lost her composure for a second.

About five minutes into Mocha's speech, gasps could be heard throughout the sound room. Women and men alike could be heard saying "oh my God," undoubtedly followed by covering their mouths with their hands.

Mocha's body began to tremble. She couldn't believe her eyes. How could this be happening? Within the next couple of minutes the video feed was joined by audio. The sounds of sexing, lovemaking, or whatever you chose to call it filled the halls and offices of Baldwin Towers. Mocha and Billy's naked bodies were slapping and clapping as if they were giving a standing ovation. Mocha could be heard telling Billy to go harder, go deeper as he obliged, pumping long and strong into her.

"Your pussy is so good," Billy could be heard exclaiming.

Mocha sat frozen in place. She couldn't move. She began to hyper-ventilate.

"I want to taste you," Mocha's voice echoed. Mocha dropped to her knees, taking the entire length of Billy's massive penis into her mouth. The sound of Mocha giving Billy head played crystal clear. There was no mistaking the two people in the video.

Something finally jolted Mocha back to life as she bolted from the communications suite. Tears streamed down her face uncontrollably. She bypassed the elevator. She didn't want to stand waiting for it while employee's gawked at her like she was on display. She took the stairs two at a time, descending from the heights of Baldwin Tower. "How fitting," she thought, because that was just where her career that she had worked long and hard for was going, down the drain.

As soon as the video began streaming throughout the company, Billy had tried to get to Mocha. First, he tried waiting on the elevator to take him up to the floor that housed the communications suite. After deciding that it was taking too long, he ran to the stairs. Billy was sprinting at top speed up the stairs.

Billy could hear another set of feet moving in the stairwell. He didn't give it much thought. His mind had been solely on getting to Mocha. He needed to protect her. Several more seconds of Billy and Mocha making their way up and down the stairs landed them face to face. Billy's heart ached as he looked at Mocha.

The pain that he saw ran deep. He reached out to her. She fell into his arms. She began sobbing with such a howl that she would have awakened the dead. Billy scooped her into his arms. He began walking back down the stairs as the love of his life tried to bury herself into his chest. By the time Billy emerged from the stairwell with Mocha in his arms, her cries had subsided. Whimpers could still be heard as he carried her across the level 1 lobby.

Workers looked and pointed. It was the highlight of the morning, day, week, month and year. Billy didn't care. His sole purpose was to get Mocha out of the building and away from the probing eyes of these employees. The valet attendant saw Billy coming and quickly sent for his car. It pulled up within minutes. Being the boss meant that he had one of the closet valet spots in the parking garage.

Billy took care as he placed Mocha into the front seat of his car, buckling her in. He crossed over to the drivers' side of the car and hopped in. Billy sped from the scene. He reached over, placing his hand in Mocha's. He lifted it to his mouth, kissing it. Billy drove to his home. It was the one place that he knew that he could shield Mocha from the rest of the world.

CHARLES

$\mathcal{C}$harles had gone up to the communications suite when the video started. He too had tried to get into the technology booth, along with the others who worked in that department. The door had been jammed pretty good. There was no way they'd be getting into that booth with a simple key. Whoever had planned this had done a good job of keeping everyone out of that booth until the entire video had finished playing.

By the time maintenance had removed the door from its hinges, the tape was done. Charles felt bad for his friend and Mocha. Both were two of the nicest people he knew. He wondered who would want to hurt and embarrass them so deeply. Charles planned to find out. As he left communications, on his way back to the Bistro, he decided to swing by Erin's office. He hadn't seen her since their dinner date last Friday.

Charles greeted Erin's secretary, asking if he could go back to her office to see her. He was shocked to learn that she wasn't coming into work that day. When he questioned Erin's secretary, she revealed that she had not spoken to Erin directly. Amy had relayed the message. Charles wondered why Amy would be passing on a message instead of Erin calling in for herself. Charles wanted answers and he wasn't going to stop until he found them. He could feel the negativity throughout the entire Baldwin complex today. It was thick as cotton.

Charles headed towards Mocha's office. He wanted to check on Mocha and question Amy about Erin's whereabouts. As he walked into Mocha's office suite, he ran into William Baldwin. Charles wasn't the only person seeking answers. He listened as Billy's father growled at Amy. He was looking for Billy and Mocha. He was giving Amy the third degree about every piece of information he sought. He almost felt bad for Amy, but got a feeling that she could handle her own. He was starting to see her in a new light. No way was she the bashful, shy woman that he had originally thought. He had a feeling she knew a lot more about the happenings going on than anybody else in this place.

As William walked past Charles, he barely spoke. He didn't care much for Charles. He actually frowned upon him. He felt that Charles was taking advantage of his son's friendship. He had originally wanted Charles to pay for the prime retail space that housed the bistro. This would have been fine with Charles. Little did William know that Charles could have paid for the space and then some extra if needed, but Charles felt that it wasn't his place to inform the old man of his financial stability. If Billy wanted his dad to know, he would have told him.

Charles walked over to Amy's desk. She stood smiling as he approached. She was ecstatic. She hadn't expected Charles to come to claim her so quickly.

"Charles," she breathed.

"Hi Amy," Charles stated.

There was an awkward silence. Charles stared, Amy continued smiling. She was ready for Charles to take her into his arms. She wanted to feel his lips pressed against hers. Charles stepped in closer to Amy. He wanted to get a better look into her eyes. He needed to see if there was any evil intent in them. Amy's heart fluttered. She assumed that Charles was leaning in for a kiss. She closed her eyes. Her lips puckered. Charles looked confused. Amy waited. She started to wonder what was taking so long for his lips to meet hers. Amy opened one eye, peeking at Charles. Charles almost laughed out loud. He would have if not for the seriousness of the situation. He tried to help her save face.

"Have you talked to Erin?" he asked.

"No," Amy said angrily, "why would you ask me that? We aren't friends."

Charles looked baffled. He had seen Amy coming from Erin's condo with his own eyes. Erin's secretary had clearly said that Amy told her Erin wouldn't be in today.

"Oh," was all that Charles could think of to say. *This chick is really screwed up*, he thought, but more importantly he wondered where Erin was. What had she done with her?

"Do you know where Mocha is?" Charles asked.

Amy wanted to scream. She was sick and tired of everyone focusing on Mocha's black ass. First Billy, then William Baldwin, and now Charles. Amy was getting agitated. It was clearly visible to Charles. He recognized this behavior all too well. He had dealt with it his entire life.

Charles had an older cousin who was diagnosed with bipolar and schizophrenia at the age of 12. His entire childhood was like walking on egg shells when she was around. No one wanted to deal with her when she'd forgotten to take her medication, especially her parents. They had sent her to live with his family because they couldn't deal with her behavior. It never ended well. Her episodes where usually followed by a brief stay in a mental hospital until they could get her medication regulated.

"So Amy, do you have family here in Houston?" Charles asked. He wanted to keep her talking to gauge where she was on a scale of 1 to 10. It was a question that the staff at the mental hospital would ask when they called for his cousin to be picked up.

Amy was caught off guard by his reference to her family. She hadn't talked to anyone in her family in over five years.

"Why?" she questioned. Charles responded in a quiet manner. He didn't want to increase her level of stress.

"I was just wondering. When we had the picnic, you didn't mention having someone to rush home to meet," he lied.

"Oh," Amy replied. "I don't have any family. It's just little old me." Amy was back to her goofy self. Charles was taken aback. The quick change in her personality was concerning.

Charles decided to try a different approach.

"I really enjoyed your company Saturday at the park. I was wondering if you wanted to maybe go out tonight," he asked.

Amy answered quickly, "yes!"

"Great," Charles added, "what's your address?"

Amy grabbed her notepad. She scribbled her address down. Her hands were shaking as she handed it to Charles.

"I'll pick you up at 7:00."

Amy screamed when the door closed. "I knew this would work," she squealed.

22

BILLY

*B*illy reached up, pushing a control on his visor. A massive, black wrought iron gate began opening. Mocha opened her eyes at the sound of the car slowing down. She'd dozed off on the ride to wherever Billy was taking her. She was initially delighted just be with him, but quickly frowned as the reality of what had just transpired at Baldwin set in. She was having the most wonderful dream. In her dream, she was sitting in her office looking over files when Billy walked in, carrying a dozen long stem purple roses, her favorite color. She wondered how he had found out about her fondness of purple. After handing the roses to her, he dropped down to one knee. Mocha almost lost her grip on the vase. Billy reached into his pocket and pulled out a velvet purple box. Flipping the top of the box open, he revealed a princess cut, lavender tinted, sapphire baguette ring.

"Will you marry me?" Billy asked. Dreams are always cut short right when you get to good part, Mocha thought. She swallowed and tensed as Billy touched her leg.

"We're home," he stated.

Mocha didn't miss the fact that Billy had said *we* are home, referring to his place as hers.

Mocha looked around the expansive beautifully landscaped lawn. It was gorgeous. It reminded Mocha of the resort where she stayed when she was on vacation two years ago in Barcelona. Billy brought the car to a stop in the circular drive. Mocha's mouth dropped open as she took in the exterior of the mansion.

Mocha knew the value of homes. Back in Dallas, it was something that her family had done to pass time and to stay motivated to reach their dreams. They would all pile in the car on Sunday afternoons to go house looking. They would pick out the best new neighborhoods. They'd pretend that the model homes were theirs. Mocha and her sister would pick out their rooms. Her dad would pretend to kick back in the media room, while her mom would be mock cooking in the ginormous kitchen. This home definitely ranked at the top of the list of any of the homes she had ever visited as a kid.

Billy hustled around to the passenger's side of the car to open the door for Mocha. She placed her hand in his as he helped her out of the car.

As she stood, he squeezed her into an embrace. He never wanted to let her go. He placed soft kisses on the top of her head. When he released her, he spoke.

"I love you Mocha. More than words can say. I am so sorry this has happened to us, but I want you to know that when you dozed off in the car, I called the security team at Baldwin. They are scouring the building for anything out of the ordinary. I have also asked them to pull the security tapes from the last two weeks and make note of any unusual behavior by any of our employee's. While we have security camera's throughout the building none of them have been placed in any offices, which means somebody deliberately taped us and used it to hurt us," Billy explained.

Only one person came to mind, "Erin," Mocha whispered.

"That's the first person I told them to check on," Billy admitted, "but she never came in to work today. I tried to reach Charles to see if he had heard from her, but he hasn't talked to her since Friday night. They've been somewhat trying to start a relationship. He doesn't believe that it was Erin. He said he was looking at another possible angle but wanted to check it out first before he gave me all the details."

"Ok, Mocha replied, "you have a nice home."

"It's alright," Billy smiled. "Let me show you around."

They walked the path leading to the front door. Billy used a touch pad to unlock the front door. She wasn't surprised. She had already recognized that Billy loved electronic gadgets. If there was a new digital version of anything, he had it.

As they walked into the foyer, Billy's phone buzzed again. He glanced at his phone. It was his father calling for the fourteenth time. Billy pushed the button to send the call directly to voicemail. The last thing he wanted was to speak with his father. Explaining his relationship with Mocha would have to wait. His first priority was ensuring that Mocha was in a good place.

He didn't care that people now knew that he was seeing Mocha—that was going come to light after his proposed to her anyway. What did bother him was that someone deliberately went to such great lengths to cause them pain.

Although Billy couldn't be sure, he had his doubts that it was Erin. He mentally made a list of workers that he had pissed off lately, but only came up with a few names. He decided to let the security team handle it. He forwarded the names to the head of security.

"Are you hungry?" Billy asked.

"Not right now," Mocha replied.

"Would you like a tour of the house?" Billy asked. Mocha nodded yes.

The foyer was of contrasting pearl whites. It was, by far, her favorite part of homes. You could tell a lot about a person by observing the texture and colors they've chosen to decorate their homes. Clearly, the home was over 14,000 square feet. It had two levels with multiple staircasings. Mocha was impressed as she entered each of the seven bedrooms, each of which had master-sized baths. There were three dining areas, three living areas, five fireplaces, two game rooms, his and her studys, an exercise room, and a wine cellar. The backyard was even more impressive. The manicured grounds contained a koi pond, swimming pool, hot tub and a rose garden.

"Now, how many people live here?" Mocha joked as they completed the tour.

"Just me and my housekeeper," Billy answered. "Melvin," he called out. Mocha hadn't known that anyone else was in the home. A few seconds later, an older gentleman appeared.

"How can I assist you sir?" the gray haired gentlemen asked.

"I'd like you to meet Mocha," Billy introduced.

"Ah, the lady who has captured Billy's heart," he replied. Billy turned red. He had no clue Melvin would be so open with Mocha. She smiled as Melvin took her hand to his lips.

"Most pleased to meet you, Miss Mocha," Melvin charmed.

Billy rolled his eyes at his housekeeper and old friend. Billy loved Melvin like he was family. He had been there for him over the years when his own father had not. Melvin was the housekeeper for Billy's family since before he could remember. Melvin was abruptly fired by Billy's father almost five years ago. It was a subject both his father and Melvin refused to discuss with him. Neither would his mother. No one other than the three of them knew what happened and they weren't talking. Melvin was all packed up and ready to move to Dallas when Billy got the idea of hiring him to be his very own housekeeper. He refused to let the man that loved him unconditional walk out of his life because of some minor disagreement with his parents. It took a lot of convincing, but eventually Melvin relinquished. Not only was Melvin his housekeeper, but he was also his confidant. He had been talking about Mocha for months to Melvin. He was the only person who knew every detail from his stalking behavior up until that dreaded video was recorded and leaked.

"Would you like something the drink?" Melvin asked.

"Do you have any juice?" Mocha answered.

"Apple, orange and grapefruit?" he asked.

"I'll have a glass of apple juice please."

"I will have that right out."

"Um, I'll have a glass too," Billy stated to Melvin's back. Mocha laughed, then attempted to stifle a yawn.

"Let's sit," he requested.

Billy sat down, pulling Mocha to the sofa. She leaned over, placing her head on his shoulder. Billy massaged her shoulders. Mocha closed her eyes. She moaned. It was just what she needed. Mocha nodded off first, quickly followed by Billy.

Melvin returned with the drinks, but quickly retreated back to the kitchen as he saw them asleep. Melvin came back with a blanket. He draped it over the two lovebirds.

"Lovely," he stated. Melvin decided to prepare a special lunch for the two of them.

A few hours later, both Billy and Mocha were still sound asleep. It gave Melvin just enough time to put the finishing touches on his creative menu. He'd outdone himself with apricot glazed grilled pork chops, baked ginger sweet potatoes, and sautéed green vegetables topped with diced almonds. For dessert, Melvin concocted grilled apricots with almond whipped cream & honey. He had just finished placing the items on the dinner table when the alarm gave one short quick sound.

Melvin looked at the security screen in the kitchen as it beeped to notify him that someone had pulled into the drive.

"Oh boy," he stated. He hadn't seen William or his wife in almost five years. While he didn't want to see them now, he knew he had to head them off before they came into the house with their no-sense.

Melvin knew very well that they would have a problem with Billy and Mocha's relationship. He'd known them practically his entire adult life, and he also knew that William was a redneck and a racist. His wife just simply followed his lead.

WILLIAM BALDWIN, II

*M*elvin swung the door open just as William had raised his hand to knock.

"Get out of my way," William barked. He brushed pass Melvin.

"Billy!" William yelled.

Melvin stood looking at Nancy. She was still the most beautiful woman he had ever known. She cast her eyes downward, hoping to break the stare that seemed to be burning a whole right through her heart.

"Billy!" William continued on his tirade.

"What the hell!" William yelled as he walked up on Mocha and Billy, each lying in the other's arms.

"Billy, get up," he demanded, "What the hell were you thinking!" he demanded. William wanted an explanation for what he saw on the monitor earlier. Billy told him that, apparently, someone has secretly taken a video of them and played it for the entire company to see in hopes of embarrassing them.

His father responded, "No shit Sherlock, that's pretty obvious." William ignored Mocha. He pretended as though she wasn't there. He couldn't believe she had screwed his son when she could have had him instead.

"What I want to know is what the hell is going on with you and this tramp?"

Billy couldn't control his reflexes. He punched his father squarely in the nose. His mother screamed. Blood gushed from his nose, splattering the pearly white décor.

"Billy," Melvin scolded, "that was not necessary. You shouldn't disrespect your father that way."

"And he shouldn't disrespect Mocha," Billy growled.

"You're just like your goddamn mother, sleeping with the fucking help," William raged.

Everything in the house went quiet at his fathers' revelation. That old cliché was right–you could literally hear a pin drop.

Billy looked at his mother, then looked at Melvin. It all made since to him now. It was what had caused his father to fire Melvin–he had slept with his mother. Billy frowned at the visual that popped into his brain. His mother, Nancy, was completely mortified. She turned and ran back out the front door.

"Nancy," Melvin called after her.

"Don't fucking call my wife's name, you lying piece of shit!" William barked at Melvin.

Melvin wanted to go after her, but he knew it would only make things worse. William stood up off the ground as blood was still gushing from his nose. He turned to Melvin yelling, "get me a fucking towel!"

Although he didn't want to do it, Melvin decided to take the high road. He walked to the linen closet to retrieve a towel. William snatched it from his hand. He pressed it against his nose as he held his head tilted to a backwards position. Mocha sat stoically throughout the entire exchange. She tried her best to fade into the background. She refused to meet her bosses gaze.

"Father, you are no longer welcome in my home. Please leave," Billy demanded.

"Mocha," William spoke directly to her, "just so you know, you're fired. You can come by tomorrow after hours to pick up all of your belongings. I'll have your secretary pack up all of your things. Mocha remained quiet.

"I can pack my own things," Mocha stated.

"Well if Mocha is fired, then I quit, and get the hell out of my house." Billy pushed his father out the door and slammed it behind him.

Mocha finally spoke, "you didn't have to do that."

Billy told her, "I'm in love with you, I plan to spend the rest my life with you, and if he can't accept our relationship, then I cannot accept him as my father."

Melvin smiled. He loved the man that Billy had grown to be. He liked to believe that he had a hand in raising him. When William was off working twelve hours a day, Melvin was the one who would bandage scraped knees, attend father-son camping trips with the boy scouts, and even love his mother like a real husband should.

Melvin quickly admonished himself for thinking inappropriately. It was true; he loved Nancy more than life itself, but their love was never meant to be. Melvin accepted his fate long ago. He knew Nancy loved him, but he also knew that she would never leave her husband to pursue a relationship with him. Seeing her today had brought back a ton of emotions. His feelings about the situation were still as raw as the day she attempted to jump off of the third story balcony of the home she shared with William. Nancy had wanted to take her own life. She was miserable being Mrs. William Baldwin, II. Melvin had walked into her private room to put up clean linens when he spotted her standing on the railing just outside the terrace doors, prepared to take her own life. When he grabbed her, she fought him tooth and nail to free herself. She wanted to complete her mission. Melvin felt himself losing control of the situation. He was afraid that she would break free from his protecting arms. He did what he thought would be the one thing that might calm her down. He took her face into his hands, leaned down, and passionately kissed away her pain. He felt Nancy relax in his arms as she matched his passion, desperately seeking solace within his masculine arms. It was the start of a beautiful forbidden relationship to which no one could ever know about.

Nancy needed Melvin. Melvin had saved her life. Had he not walked into the room that dreadful day, she would have been just a distant memory at this point in her family's life. Nancy was sure that William would have remarried by now. He had needs, needs that she could no longer fulfill even if she wanted to. His appetite for exotic beautiful women had left her without so much as an ounce of passion from William since their first five years of marriage. William had surrounded himself with those type of women every chance that he got—his secretaries, personal assistants, personal shoppers, hair stylists, groomers, all exotic beautiful women, all of whom he had slept with throughout their marriage.

After hiring a private investigator to get the proof of what she already knew, she was fed up. The investigator had followed William for over six months. Within that time frame he had sex with over a hundred women. One thing was for sure, although his mouth ran rampant concerning issues surrounding race, he did not discriminate when it came to having his needs met. African American, Asian, and Latina women were all accounted for.

Initially, Nancy was ready to accept the fact that her husband had cheated on her, but when she found out the depths to which his cheating had escalated, she couldn't play the good wife by just accepting her fate. When she approached William about her findings, he laughed in her face, calling her a fool. He'd told her she didn't have to waste well-earned money on a private investigator. He laughed again, telling her that she could have simply asked him and he would have told her the truth. The truth was, as he put it, he hadn't been in love with her since she'd had Billy and refused to lose her pregnancy weight. He added that even if she decided to lose the weight now, it would not matter. He was so into his exotic beauty collection that he never wanted to have sex with her again, ever. After spewing those evil words to her, he simply walked out the door, saying that he was going over to Asha's house so that he could be properly satisfied by his new hot young secretary.

"I'm so glad this is finally out in the open. Now, I can stop making up all these silly excuses about working late and business trips. Don't wait up for me," he said over his shoulder as he walked out the door."

The next day was the day that Melvin saved her from herself. They made sweet passionate love all day, never uttering one single word. From that day forward, she and Melvin were inseparable, at least when William wasn't around. They'd secretly count down the days until his next business trip so that they could be together as a pretend family. She, Melvin, and her boys traveled together just as a real family would. Most people believed that her kids were his biological children. William actually encouraged Melvin to spend as much time as possible with his family. He wanted free reign to do as he pleased. William encouraged vacations, theme parks, and even visits to his in-laws.

It was the perfect set-up for his philandering ways without having his wife nag him about spending time with the family. Nancy and Melvin gave him exactly what he wanted, because in turn, they were able to remain secret lovers right under her husband's nose. That was exactly the case, until William decided to return home two days early from one of his fake business trips.

He had fallen ill in Morocco. His young flavor of the month refused to nurse him back to health. She had left him to fend for himself as she shopped and partied all over town. When William decided to go look for her later that evening in the hotel lobby, he found her in a dark corner of the hotels bar making out with one of the bartenders. William had never before been as embarrassed as he had when the bellhop pointed her out to him. He picked up his pride and flew home to Nancy so that she could tend to her so-called husband.

When William walked into their bedroom, Nancy was straddled atop Melvin riding him like she was in the rodeo. The emotions she was emitting caused a boil in William that she didn't think was possible. Nancy was in the middle of proclaiming Melvin to be ten times better at sexing her than her husband. William lost it. The couple nearly jumped out of their skin at the primal roar unleashed from her husband's mouth. William charged at Melvin, throwing his entire body into him just as he stood from the bed. Nancy screamed. Here she was trying to stop her husband from killing her lover with his bare hands, but also getting a laugh at the fact that William was jealous and Melvin was dangling all over the place naked as a jaybird. Melvin was the bigger of the two men and could have very easily put William flat on his ass, but he chose the high road and retreated to his quarters located in east wing of the house.

That night was the last time she had seen her lover. William had forced her hand, threatening to expose her relationship with the "housekeeper" to every tabloid magazine that he knew. Nancy hadn't wanted to break things off with Melvin, let alone fire him, but she felt that she hadn't a choice in the matter. After Melvin left their home, Nancy once again fell into a deep depression, only this time, she had the memories of her time with Melvin to keep her from wanting to leave this world.

She was ecstatic to learn that Billy had hired him to work at his home. While she could have easily pretended to visit her son to see her former lover, she never did. She didn't take the threats from her husband idly. If he said he was going to do something, you could bet money on it that he truly was. It was one of those personal characteristics that led her to marry him in the first place. Now that trait was biting her in the ass.

CHARLES

*C*harles spent most of the morning scouring the video footage with the security team. Their eyes had become weak from looking through so much tape. Baldwin Towers had more than 313,609 square foot of office space. Looking at each hallway, lounge, garage parking space, and the outside perimeter wouldn't be an easy task as they searched for the needle in the haystack, but it finally paid off. An hour after Billy and Mocha arrived at Baldwin on Saturday, Amy walked into Baldwin as well.

The security team had no clue that this was what he was looking for. They assumed that, as Mocha's secretary, she was there to help her boss. Charles followed her on the tape until she turned into her office area. He was definitely going to suggest to Billy that they needed to invest in office cameras as well. He didn't think it would be such a hard sell given their current situation.

Charles decided to go backwards from that date to see if Amy could be seen in any other parts of the video. He came upon some footage of Amy getting out of Erin's car in front of Baldwin. He quickly jotted down the day and time shown on the monitor. He continued to work his way back in the footage. Another section of the tape had shown Amy and Erin talking in front of the elevators.

"Don't know her that well my ass," Charles mumbled.

Charles phone rang as he was wrapping of his amateur detective work. He stepped into the hallway to speak privately to Billy. Charles relayed a few of his suspicions to Billy. He didn't want to fill him in on everything until he was sure. The last thing he wanted was to falsely accuse someone of wrongdoing. Billy told his friend to let him know if he needed anything. He also told him to be careful, and that if his instincts proved to be correct, they could potentially be dealing with a crazed psychopath.

Charles walked back into the security booth. The monitors where now showing in real time. He watched as Amy carried a box, purse, and jacket towards the elevator. When he saw her, he decided to rush to the parking garage. He assumed she was leaving for the day. He already had her address, but he wanted to see if she made any stops on her way home.

Charles raced down the stairs. He made it to his car just as Amy was entering the parking garage. He slipped into his car sliding down in the front seat to keep her from seeing him. She walked past his car slightly glancing and smiling in his cars direction. He wondered if she had seen him. Within minutes, she was exiting the garage.

Charles started his car and followed from a safe distance. He laughed at how horrible of a driver she was. She darted in and out of traffic. He had to cut off a few cars himself just to keep up with her. After 20 minutes, she swung her car into a driveway of smaller style, but elegant home. He was surprised at how neat and manicured the lawn appeared. He took her for the type of girl who could care less about a well-maintained look. She exited the car, half bouncing and skipping into the house. Before she closed the door, he saw her bend to pick up a cat.

"Well that's just great," Charles uttered. He hated cats with a passion. It stemmed from when he was a kid and his great aunt's cat, Buttermilk, had attacked him without warning–at least that's what he told his aunt. The truth was that he had tortured that poor cat for hours, pulling its tale. He guessed he had pulled one too many times, because Buttermilk perched, hissed, and attempted to scratch his eyes out.

From that day forward, he never let his path cross with another cat again.

This was one time that he would have to put his fear aside. If he was right, many lives depended on it. Charles decided to pull his car further done the street just in case Amy was lurking out the window. He walked back up the street, being careful not to be seen. He was able to get a good look into the front room. The first thing he saw was the ugly cat. Charles swore he could hear the cat hissing through the window. He moved towards the back of the house and almost pancaked to the ground as Amy brushed by the window in nothing but her birthday suit.

He frowned at the sight of her naked body. He assumed she had music playing in the background as she swayed her hips from side to side. He almost regurgitated as she bent over attempting to twerk. The jiggling of her cheeks was something that no one should ever have to see. After a few minutes, Amy disappeared into what Charles assumed was her bedroom. He seized the opportunity. He walked into the back-yard and onto the porch. It was a longshot, but he tried turning the doorknob just for the sake of trying. When the handle twisted, he was happy for his stroke of good luck. As he opened the door, he could hear what sounded like water running in a shower. Charles tip toed throughout the house. He did quick scan of each room. While he was hoping to find Erin in one of them, he was also hoping that he was wrong and wouldn't find her there.

Nervous jitters began to set in when Charles reached a room that was locked. *Why would anyone who lived by themselves lock a room in their own home*, he thought. Charles flipped open his pocket knife that was attached to his keys. They jingled a bit, but doubted Amy could have heard them because of the loudness of the water running in the shower. After a few pokes, the lock turned with ease. Charles was proud of himself. He still had the touch. He had learned how to jimmy a lock open when he was twelve years old at summer camp. When he opened the door, his mouth hung open. There were scores and scores of pictures plastered across the wall. He knew something had been amiss, but he had no idea that Mocha was the target of Amy's delusional behavior. Charles looked from wall to wall. It's like she had been stalking Mocha. Pictures were at various places around the city, all of them were candid shots. Some of them had been cut out. Charles assumed that Billy must have been in the poses that were cut up. Charles noticed what looked like a picture album sitting on the dresser. It caught his attention because of the words scribbled across the front. It read, "stupid ass bitches." Charles picked up the album, and just as he was about to open it, he heard the water shut off in the bathroom. He quickly placed the album back in its place. He quietly closed the door and turned to walk away. Before he could make it to the back door, the bathroom door swung open.

MOCHA

*M*ocha wondered what Billy's father was referring to when he mentioned sleeping with the help. She was mortified to be referred to in that way, but his mother had to be embarrassed to the hilt. After all the work she had put in at Baldwin, she couldn't believe that her boss would refer to her simply as the help. And to add insult to injury, she'd been fired.

Mocha didn't know what her next move would be, but she was glad that she didn't have to face it alone. Billy had just told her he planned to spend the rest of his life with her. It made things only a little less to bear. She didn't think she could ever walk back through the doors of Baldwin Enterprises again. Mocha had always been a private person. To have her personal affairs broadcast throughout the company was something she didn't think she could recover from.

Mocha gave serious thought to who might try to hurt her this way. She still hadn't ruled Erin out but trusted Billy when he said that he didn't think it was her. She didn't know why he had such faith in her after the way she responded to them having dinner together a while back, but Billy explained how Erin had just started dating Charles. They were totally focused on each other.

"Oh my God!" Mocha exclaimed. Mocha was so deep in thought

that she had forgotten that Billy was in the room. He too had been mentally processing the events of the day, although he was wondering more about his father's rude comments to his mother, and to whom his father could be referring to as the help that his mother had apparently had an affair with.

"What is it?" Billy responded.

"Amy," Mocha exhaled.

"Your secretary?" Billy questioned

"Yes!"

"What about her?" he asked.

"She has been acting strange lately and giving off these weird vibes, not to mention she has unquestionable access to my office. She could have easily placed a hidden camera in my office without me knowing," Mocha explained.

"She is a weird one. Charles told me how she just happened to show up in the park where he had planned a picnic for him and Erin. Later, he said that he saw her coming from Erin's condo. When he asked her about Erin, she acted like she barely knew her," he added.

Mocha pondered what Billy had just relayed to her. She tried to rack her brain to remember what Amy's background had been when she hired her almost two years ago. Nothing was popping into her mind at the moment.

"Charles is worried, because he hasn't spoken to Erin since their date last weekend. A little boy who lives in the condo across the hall from Erin told him that he hasn't seen Erin since last Thursday, but that Amy has been going in and out of Erin's apartment all week-end," Billy continued with this new information. Mocha's mind was turning a mile a minute. She didn't think any of this was a coincidence.

"Charles asked Amy to go out with him so that he could get a look around her place. Of course, she happily agreed. He is supposed to swing by to pick her up around 7:00, but he said he was purposely going to show up 30 minutes early to try to catch her off guard," Billy stated, "he is really worried about Erin.

"After hearing all of this, so am I," Mocha said. Billy loved that she was concerned about Erin, even though she and Erin had gotten off to a bad start. It showed her compassionate side.

"Is he taking someone with him?" she asked.

"No, he said he can handle Amy."

"I'm not sure if that's wise," Mocha worried.

"Charles is smart and very athletic. If things get weird, he can handle himself," Billy explained.

"Ok," Mocha replied, sighing as she thought about just being fired. She had worked tirelessly to prove herself in a male dominated profession. All of her hard work had been washed away in the blinking of an eye. She couldn't believe the events of the day. She could truly say this has been the worst day of her entire life.

Billy walked over to console her. He could feel the shift in her mood. He wanted to assure her that everything would be ok. He held her close and told her just that. Mocha had never been the type of person who believed in fairy tales, but Billy made her change her thought patterns with ease. If he said that things would turn out good, then she would trust in him. *Sometimes fairytales do come true*, she thought.

Melvin reentered the room, announcing that the meal was ready to be served.

"I was wondering what smelled so good," Billy interjected.

Melvin rattled off the dishes that he'd prepared. Billy and Mocha's stomachs rumbled, signaling their excitement for the tasty entrees. By time they finished, both had overdone it, stuffing forkfuls of food into their mouths. Melvin thought that neither must have eaten in days.

"That was so good Melvin," Mocha moaned. Billy concurred. Billy nodded at Melvin, giving him the signal that tonight would indeed be the night that he surprised Mocha. Even before the wicked events of the day, he and Billy had planned this night. The pilot was on standby, waiting for Melvin's call.

The terrace was the most romantic space in the home. Billy had arranged every detail for this special day weeks ago. They were on schedule for everything. Billy only hoped he would be granted his wish.

"If you two would like to retreat to the terrace, I will serve you tea out there. The evening sun is setting, and it's casting the most beautiful orange hues across the property." Mocha smiled at Melvin while Billy made a goofy face. Melvin had only just met Mocha, but Billy could tell that he approved of his choice for a mate. Melvin nodded back at Billy to signal that everything was on schedule.

Billy pulled out Mocha's chair. She sat with her back cattycornered to the impressive landscape. *Melvin was right*, Mocha thought, it was absolutely beautiful. Melvin placed tea in front of both Billy and Mocha.

"If there is nothing else, sir, I will be retiring to my quarters," Melvin affirmed.

"Thank you for everything, Melvin," Billy responded.

"My pleasure," Melvin retorted.

The couple took in the beauty and slight cool breeze without words. In the distance, they could hear a slight humming sound. It was some type of buzz. The noise grew louder as Mocha looked to see where the sound had originated.

ERIN

*E*rin had all but given up. It had been an entire day now that Amy hadn't been back to feed her, clean her or just simply talk like she had done when she initially started holding her captive. Erin didn't want to die like this, but was quickly losing hope. She told herself she had to accept her fate. She wondered if this was her karma for all that she had ever done wrong over the years.

Erin wasn't a bad person, at least not intentionally. Sure, she acted like a Prima Donna most of the time, and she had fucked up her ex-boyfriends property when she found out that he had been using her, but did that constitute being treated like an animal? She never imagined the homely-looking secretary would be the cause of her demise.

She longed for her parents. She had spent years trying to keep her distance from them, even refusing to live in the same city because she wanted to be truly on her own. She wondered how they would accept her death, Erin being their only child. She had hated their overprotectiveness; now she longed for it. She would give anything to have them walk through her door at this moment. Tears began to stream as the thought of never seeing them again. "I need you mommy," she said aloud.

Her thoughts moved to Charles. She had finally found the person that she was sure to be her knight in shining armor, but she would be deprived of exploring what could have been.

Erin's body had grown weak. She had never gone two days without eating in all of her life. She wondered how long a person could live without food. She wished she could turn off her thoughts. The silence was killing her. Between the two, if she didn't die soon, she would surely go insane.

She started to hum. She had read that someone once kept their sanity while being trapped in a room by humming songs. After ten minutes, she couldn't think of a single song to hum. Erin's temperament vacillated just like the wind. She smiled as thoughts of Charles entered her mind. She thought about her last time seeing him. She thought about his attempt to reach out to her that were intercepted by Amy. She would have loved to go running in the park with him. The picnic would have been an added bonus. She would have definitely tried to seduce him on the picnic blanket in front of God and everybody. All eyes would have been on them. Erin's spirits began to perk up a bit. There was still hope. As long as she was still breathing, there was still hope.

"That's it," she thought, "I have to think about my future. It's the key to my survival," but just as quickly as her mood heightened, it plummeted when she looked towards her bedroom window. The sun was setting. Erin's breathing began to increase. The darkness would once again wreak havoc on her emotional state. Daylight inspired hope. She could listen to the rumblings of her neighbors as they went about their daily lives. She could imagine greeting each of them as she hustled to her car. She would see Mr. and Mrs. Kampi as they kissed goodbye before he sped off to his job at the post office. She'd hear Ms. Davies as she yelled to her children to hurry before they missed the school bus. She would flirt with Kevin Andrews while he walked back to his condo from retrieving his mail. All those interactions that she normally took for granted provided her with the slightest smile, but during the stillness of the night, her thoughts would drift to Amanda Berry, Gina DeJesus, and Michelle Knight. She prayed that she wouldn't have to endure years of captivity as those young women did.

Erin hated her plight and wouldn't wish it upon anyone, but in a weird way, she envied those women because at least they had each other. She knew that it was a selfish thing to think, but this ordeal had caused her to lose all rationalization. She thought of Elisabeth Fritzl. Her father had held her captive for 24 years in a makeshift basement below their family home but even she had someone to talk with. Her father had repeatedly raped her, causing her to bear seven of his children.

That's sick Erin. You are comparing yourself to women who have gone through years of being raped and held in captivity. At least you haven't been raped or beaten. And your father would never harm one single hair on your head. Erin continued referring to herself in third person. *Erin, you have to hold it together. Your mom and dad raised you to be strong person. Hell, you were a girl scout, for Christ sake.*

I must have missed the meeting on "How to Survive Being Kidnapped and Held Captive," Erin laughed at her little joke. The laugh was short lived as she immediately burst into tears. She started her nightly ritual. 1, 2, 3, 4, 5… Counting kept the negative thoughts at bay. She would eventually drift off to sleep. Each morning she would try to remember the highest number she reached before she entered dreamland. Last night the number had been 10,692. She was sure it was higher but that was the last one that she could remember. 899, 900, 901, 902, 903…

CHARLES

*C*harles' eyes nearly popped out of his head. Amy must have heard him in the room. Without waiting to see who was trespassing in her personal space, she attacked. Shampoo still in her hair and burning her eyes, she brought the knife that she held high over her head down with a quick motion, slicing through Charles' flesh. It happened so fast that he didn't have time to dodge the razor sharp blade. He groaned at the pain while dropping to his knees. "Amy," he called out. Amy panicked at the sound of the man's voice calling out to her. She recognized the voice. She grabbed a towel to wipe the suds from her eyes. "Oh my God," she responded, "Charles!"

Blood was oozing from his body. Amy's nursing skills kicked in without her realizing it. Her mind transported her back to her early days of working in the emergency room. It had been her first job after graduating with her Bachelor's degree in nursing. She had to try to save her patient. The first thing she wanted to do was to control the hemorrhage. Once she did that, she looked at the length and the size of the knife blade and the trajectory that it followed. Charles was breathing but going in and out of consciousness. She was working feverously to stabilize him. She couldn't lose her future husband. "Honey, I am so sorry. I had no idea it was you," she spoke. "But I am going to fix you up as good as new." Charles moaned. The pain was blinding.

"I'll get you something for pain," Amy explained as she ran to the kitchen. Charles was sore and experiencing excruciating pain, but tried his best to crawl towards the backdoor. The phone in his pocket buzzed. Amy heard it and noticed that it was coming from a different direction in the house than where Charles had been lying in front of the bathroom. For the first time, Amy began wondering what Charles was doing in her home. He wasn't supposed to be her for another hour. She frowned as she thought about how he had gotten into her home. She looked at the front door. It was still bolted shut. She walked towards the back door. She noticed the door wasn't locked. She looked down at Charles, who had apparently lost consciousness again. His phoned continued to buzz. Amy reached into his pocket removing the phone. Billy's picture appeared on the screen. A few seconds after it stopped, one quick buzz sounded, signaling that he had received a voice message. Amy pushed the listen button. She wanted to hear what Billy had to say.

"Hey Charles, its' Billy. I am just checking in on you. Were you able to find out any more information about Amy? Do you really believe that she is responsible for all of this mess? Have you heard from Erin yet? Call me back as soon as possible. Let me know that you are ok."

When the message stopped, Amy screamed. She started to rant.

"You only asked me out to try to get information about me," she yelled. Amy leaned back and kicked her foot full force into Charles' chest. He groaned. Amy was heading towards a full psychotic melt down. She marched around Charles lethargic body.

"Why are you attacking me," she implored. "I wasn't trying to kill him," she spoke. "No, I wasn't," Amy continued her conversation with the voice speaking in her head. It had been years since she'd heard it. It was condescending. "I am not stupid," she growled. "I can kill him," Amy continued. "Stop it! Stop telling me what to do," Amy yelled placing her hands over her ears. "La, la, la," she sang, rocking back and forth as to drown out the voice in her head. "Leave me alone," she cried.

Charles listened, as Amy battled with the demon in her head. He was growing weaker by the minute. If Amy didn't kill him herself, he would surely die from the amount of blood he was losing.

Amy paced the floor. She was in a full psychotic trance. She paid less attention to Charles, focusing 100 % on the voice. Charles used it as an opportunity to inch his was closer to the door. It was now or never. He had to get out of the twilight zone. At this moment, he was thankful for the demonic voice that was talking to her. It kept her attention long enough for him to make it to the door. Amy was fully consumed with trying to make the voice understand. Charles was able to get out of the door without Amy noticing. As he rounded the house, he could still hear her verbally arguing with the voice. As fast as his wounds would allow, Charles hurried down the street. When he reached his car, he collapsed into the front seat.

BILLY

*B*illy watched as Mocha careened her neck to try to get a better look at the sound coming from the east side of the terrace. Finally, an airplane came into clear view. It was an odd looking plane. Billy smiled as he observed Mocha watching the aircraft. Mocha only realized it was a skywriting plane when the pilot started to make a loop. She spelled out each letter as the pilot enjoyed the adrenaline of flying his plane in circles. When he had gotten to M-O-C, Mocha covered her mouth. She watched as her name lit up the sky. She looked at Billy. He pointed up to the sky. Mocha looked, she saw the word will. She looked back at Billy, who was now holding a small box in his hand. Mocha was beyond excited. When she took a final look at the sky. The pilot had finished. *Mocha will you marry me* was floating high above. Billy dropped down to one knee. He opened the box revealing a princess cut diamond.

"Mocha, will you please do me the honor of being my wife?"

"Yes, absolutely," she answered.

Within minutes, the plane appeared again. Mocha looked up to see weighted balloons dropping from the plane. It was the prettiest thing Mocha had ever seen falling from the sky. After dropping the balloons, the plane began writing again. Now floating in the sky were the words, *she said yes*.

Billy picked Mocha up, swinging her around. She had just made him the happiest man in the world.

"Billy," he heard Melvin call out. Both Billy and Mocha turned to look in his direction. Melvin clearly appeared distressed. He asked Billy if he could speak with him for a minute. Billy knew it must be important. Otherwise, Melvin wouldn't have interrupted him at such an important time.

When Billy returned to Mocha, he told her everything that Melvin stated. Mocha covered her mouth for the second time that night, but this time, it wasn't for a happy occasion. Charles was in the hospital.

"If you don't mind, I really need to get to the hospital. I'm the only family that Charles has got," Billy said.

"*We* need to get to the hospital," Mocha corrected, "and now he has me too."

On the ride over, Mocha asked more questions than Billy could answer. Melvin had only been told that Charles had been found slumped over in his car. Someone called the police. When they arrived, Charles was unconscious. The police saw the pool of blood and called for paramedics.

When Billy and Mocha arrived at the hospital, they were directed to a private family room. A chaplain came in to explain that Charles was in grave condition. He had lost a lot of blood. He was in surgery at the moment, and the doctors would come out to give them more details soon. When the Chaplain exited the room, tears began streaming down Billy's face. Charles was more than just his best friend. He was the one person on earth that knew him better than anyone else. He was his friend, confidant, and brother.

"I am so sorry," Mocha consoled. She sat next to Billy holding his hands.

"I can't lose him," Billy stated. Mocha didn't respond. She didn't want to give him false hope if there wasn't any. She allowed him the chance to just talk. Some people need to just talk as a way to remain calm.

"Is there anybody you want me to call?" Mocha asked.

"No," Billy mumbled.

"What about your parents," Mocha questioned.

Billy nodded his head yes.

Mocha took Billy's phone. She dialed his mothers' cellular number. She quickly explained what they knew. His mother said they were coming right over.

When the door to the family room opened, they both stood assuming it would be the doctors with news about Charles' condition, but it was a uniformed officer and another man who appeared to be a detective. After trading pleasantries, the officers got right down to business. They wanted to know if we knew of anyone who would have wanted to hurt Charles. Billy immediately shook his head no. His friend didn't have any enemies.

The officer went on to explain where they had found Charles. He told them that there was a trail of blood leading down the street. They assumed that Charles was stabbed somewhere other than in his car. Seeing that he was in a neighborhood, they suspected one of the homes on the street, but since he had dragged his body through puddles of water they were unable to determine which home. Billy was stumped. He had a hard time concentrating. His mind was solely on his friend's survival.

Things finally started clicking with Mocha.

"Wait," she blurted. Everyone turned to her.

"I don't know how relevant this is," Mocha stated.

The officer responded. "Any information may possibly be a good tip, no matter how small you think it is."

"Charles was doing a little detective work," she said. "We had an incident over at Baldwin Towers. There were a lot a strange things happening, things that didn't quite add up. It appeared that everything was pointing towards my secretary, Amy. She befriended Charles, and tonight he was going over to her house to try to see if he could get any more information."

Billy hit his hand to his head. In his distraught state, he had forgotten that Charles was checking out Amy as a suspect. A wave a guilt hit him for not discouraging his friend from investigating his situation. Billy now felt that he should have been the one checking out Amy. His friend wouldn't be fighting for his life it he had taken on his own responsibilities.

"Where does this Amy live?" the detective asked.

"I don't have the exact address, but I know she lives on Sage Brush in the North Houston. The detective scribbled the information down before informing them that was the street on which Charles was found.

"Oh God," Billy breathed.

The officer used his radio to call back in to dispatch at the station. He asked them to locate the physical address for Amy. He provided the information that Mocha had supplied. It didn't take long for them to get the needed information.

The officers hurried out after providing them with business cards to call if they thought of any new information.

29

AMY

*A*my's psychotic episode lasted nearly an hour. By the time she calmed, her house looked as though a tornado had hit it. The table in the breakfast nook was flipped. The glass mirrors throughout the house were smashed. Her sofa was ripped to shreds with a knife sticking out of the back. The television screen and computer monitor was busted.

By the time Amy remembered what had happened that led to her episode, Charles was no longer in her home. She followed the blood trail from her back door around the house and to the front yard. Once there her eyes were immediately drawn to a scene down the street. Police cars and an ambulance were in sight. Her neighbors lined the street, trying to get a better look at what had taken place.

Amy didn't need an explanation. She could see Charles vehicle. She could see him on the stretcher as they placed it in the back of the ambulance. Panic set in as she got the impulse to flee. She had no intention of sticking around to see if he would survive her attack. She felt that she wasn't the type of woman who could do prison time. As much as she loved Houston, she could no longer call it home.

Amy stepped back into her home without being noticed. She calmly walked to the hallway closet. She pulled her already packed "quick getaway" suitcase out. It contained clothes, shoes, toiletries, and the cash she needed to start over in a new city. She pulled the car keys out of a side pocket on the suitcase. She had planned for this day long ago. While she loved Houston and wanted to stay, she always knew that it was a possibility that she would have to pick up and move at a minutes notice. As motivation, she always used the quote, "if you fail to plan, you are planning to fail," and failure was not an option. If she failed, it would constitute jail time. Amy walked into the garage. She pulled the car cover off her second car. This car would carry her to a new city and new life. While the police would be looking for the car that she drove to work at Baldwin Towers every day, she would be cruising to some place that she had yet to decide.

Amy thought for a moment as she backed out of her driveway. North, South, East, West; she would pick a direction and decide where to drop her bags on a whim.

"Surprise me," she said to her car.

30

ERIN

*E*rin had fallen to sleep right around the 9996 mark. Sleep had come much sooner for her tonight. She was grateful. Erin hadn't dreamt much since her ordeal began. She had fallen asleep after thinking of her parents, so it only made logical sense to her that she would dream about them. Erin smiled as she slept. Her parents had rushed into her room. Her smiles rapidly turned in to a frown when she saw the look of concern on her mothers' face. Erin wondered what could be troubling her. She looked to her dad. He had an equally concerned look on his face.

"I knew something was wrong," she heard her mother say. *What's wrong*, Erin thought.

Her parents rushed to the bed, each sitting on opposite sides of Erin. She saw tears in her father's eyes. She had never before seen him cry. It wasn't until her father leaned over that she realized she wasn't dreaming at all. Her father was reaching over to untie her hands. Her mother carefully removed the duct tape from her mouth, trying her best to not cause Erin any unnecessary pain. Her mother could no longer hold back her tears. They were free flowing. Erin joined in as tears flooded her face.

"We need to call the police," her mother implored.

Erin's father moved to the other room to make the call.

"How did you know?" Erin asked her mother.

"A mothers' intuition," she replied, "I knew something was wrong. I felt it in my heart. When I couldn't reach you after a few days, we decided to take the next flight out of Boston to come check on you, and I am so glad we did. Lord knows how long you could have survived like this. You've lost so much weight. How long have you been tied up like this, she asked?"

"I don't know," Erin replied. I lost track of time after a couple of days.

"Who did this to you," her mom asked. Before she could answer, two paramedics walked into the room. They immediately began to take Erin's vital signs. Her parents stepped into the living area to speak with a police officer about how they found there daughter tied up. They couldn't provide any other information. Erin's little neighbor from across the hall stuck his head into the door. He asked if Erin was okay. Her parents responded that she would be. He explained that he had been worried about her, because he hadn't seen her in a while. He also told the officers about Charles and how they were trying find Erin. He mentioned Amy and how she had been going in and out of Erin's apartment. The officer's ears perked up at the mention of the name Amy. He had just heard the name come across the dispatch radio, just before entering the condominium parking lot. The officer tried to get as much information as possible from the little boy. The officer agreed to the paramedics' request of interviewing Erin after she had gained a little bit more strength.

The paramedics decided that Erin needed to be transported to the hospital for further evaluations. Erin was grateful that this ordeal was finally over. She couldn't wait to send Amy to jail for causing her so much pain. Erin was even more elated to hear that Charles had been trying to find her. The first thing she wanted to do when she reached the hospital was to find a phone to call Charles. She wanted to let him know that she would be fine.

Erin's mother would not let her out of her sight. She rode in the back of the ambulance with her, while her father sat in the passenger seat in the front of the ambulance. The ambulance pulled up into the emergency room entrance. The paramedics unloaded the gurney with Erin in it.

As they were rolling her through the emergency room doors, Erin heard someone call her name. When she looked to see who it was, she was shocked.

"Mr. and Mrs. Baldwin, what are you doing here?" Erin asked.

"We are here to visit one of Billy's friends. But more importantly, what happened to you?" Mrs. Baldwin asked.

Erin had briefly worked with William on a few projects and met his wife at several company functions. They both knew that, at one point, she wanted a relationship with their son. They were both all for it, but Billy was the one that needed convincing.

"It's a long story," Erin answered.

"You look pale and weak," Mr. Baldwin added.

"Well we better get going," Mrs. Baldwin stated. "We will have Billy to come down to check on you once Charles comes out of surgery."

"Charles!" Erin panicked.

"Yes, Billy's friend Charles was stabbed in his chest tonight. Do you know Charles?" William asked. Erin shook her head yes as tears began to collect in her eyes.

"Oh honey, I didn't mean to upset you," Nancy said.

"Is he going to be ok?" Erin questioned.

"We can't really say because we haven't been up to see him yet, but Mocha sounded calm when she called us to come to the hospital.

"I want to go with you," Erin stated. Erin tried to get off the gurney, but she was quickly stopped by her mother.

"You can't go to see anyone just yet ma'am. We have to get you evaluated," the paramedic added.

Erin began breathing roughly. "I have to see Charles," she repeated.

"Erin you have to calm down," her mother told her.

"Does she have asthma?" he asked.

"She did when she was a little girl, but now it only flares up when she gets extremely emotional," Erin's dad responded.

"Let's get her to trauma room 3, the emergency room nurse stated as they began wheeling Erin through the double doors.

"I take it you all are Erin's parents?" William asked.

"And you are the owner of Baldwin Enterprises?"

"What happened to her, if you don't mind us asking? We've grown quite fond of Erin since she started working at Baldwin," William inquired.

"From what we can piece together, someone named Amy tied Erin up and held her captive for about a week. She would still be there tied up if it wasn't for my wife. She just had a feeling that something was amiss."

"After we couldn't get her on the phone for a couple of days, we decided to come check on her," Amy's mother finished. The Baldwin's left to check in with their son. Erin's parents stayed by her side.

31

CHARLES

*T*he surgery room nurse was barking out instructions. Every person in the room listened intently to what she had to say. It was like she was running a mini-army camp.

"The victim sustained a single stab wound to the left chest in the mid axillary line, just below the level of the nipple. He was transported to our emergency department by Houston EMS. He was noted as not being awake or alert throughout the entire transport."

"Details," she continued, *"past Medical/Surgical History: Asthma. Family History: Non-significant. Medications: Inhalers as needed. Allergy: No Known Drug Allergy"*

"Cardiac monitors, blood pressure-cuff and oxygen saturation probes are all in place on the patient." She continued by rattling off his vital signs.

"Heart rate- 90/min. Blood Pressure- 130/70. Respiratory rate 25.Temperature- 97 F."

"Everything looks good," the doctor added. "Let's get to work. It looks like he has a tracheobronchial injury. It appears to be 2.5 cm of the carina. There's some minor damage to the great vessels. We need to perform a bronchoscopy. Let's preserve his blood supply. A monofilament suture with knots tied on the outside needs to be completed."

* * *

CHARLES WAS NOW COMFORTABLY RESTING in his room. The surgical procedures were successful. Mocha, Billy, and his parents were still in the waiting room. As soon as Charles regained consciousness, they would be allowed to visit with him.

Billy and his father still had not spoken one word to each other. Mocha talked quietly with Nancy. William continued to give her the evil eye when Billy wasn't looking. Mocha ignored his rudeness. The tension in the room was thick.

"Oh my lord," Nancy exclaimed. "Is that what I think it is?" she stated. She pointed to the huge engagement ring weighing down Mocha's ring finger. All eyes focused on Mocha. She didn't know how to respond. It wasn't the way that she had wanted to inform her future in-laws about her and Billy's engagement.

Billy walked over to Mocha. He held out his hand to her. She stood. He placed a kiss on her cheek.

"Mother, Father, I asked Mocha to marry me today. I love this woman with all my heart. She has graciously agreed to be my wife."

Nancy smiled. She was happy for her son. William on the hand turned beet red. Everyone waited for him to spew his nonsense.

"You will not marry this woman," William growled, "the Baldwin's have a strong blood line, and we are going to keep it that way.

"You mean the Baldwin's have an all-white blood line and you want to keep it that way," Billy countered.

"If that's the way you want to put it, so be it. But you are not marrying her, William demanded."

"Watch me," Billy stated.

"If you marry her, I will disinherit you," William scolded.

Billy threw his fathers' words back in his face, "if that's the way you want to do it, so be it."

"You will regret the day you spoke those words," William said.

"I doubt it," Billy responded. William walked towards the door. Nancy walked over to Billy and Mocha.

"I am so happy for both of you," she admitted.

"Nancy," William said sternly, "we are leaving." William walked out the door, not waiting for his wife.

"You'd better go mom, before he blows a gasket." Nancy smiled and followed her husband out of the door. The door opened. Nancy walked back in the room.

"Son, I forgot to tell that when we were on our way up here, we passed by the emergency room. Erin was being admitted to the hospital."

"What happened?" Billy asked. He was concerned and wanted to be able to give Charles all the information he could about Erin.

"I don't have all the details," she answered, "but her parents were with her and they mentioned something about Erin being held captive by some lady who worked at Baldwin." Billy and Mocha looked at each other.

"Did they say what the lady's name was?"

"They did, but I can't remember. I think it started with an A."

"Was it Amy?" Mocha asked.

"I believe it was. Do you know her?"

"She is my secretary," Mocha told her. "We think she's the one who also did this to Charles."

When the door opened, they assumed it would be William, but it was Melvin. He had come to check on Charles. Nancy and Melvin stood looking at each other, trying to decide what to say. The awkward silence was interrupted by the nurse. She informed them that Charles was awake. He was asking about someone named Erin. They all filed out of the room, walking towards Charles' room. Nancy said her good-byes once again. Melvin asked if he could walk her to the elevator. She agreed.

Billy and Mocha walked into Charles room.

"If you wanted a break, all you had to do was ask. You didn't have to go jumping in front of a knife," Billy joked. Charles laughed and grimaced from the pain at the same time.

"I can definitely say that Amy is off her rocker and I would bet that she was the one who was responsible for the hidden camera in your office," Charles stated.

Charles filled them in on what he had discovered inside of Amy's locked room at her house. He told them how, after she stabbed him, she went on some kind of psychotic tirade. That was the only thing that allowed him to escape. He asked if the police had arrested her yet. Billy told him that the police left the hospital going over to her place, but that they hadn't heard any news yet.

Billy told Charles as much as he knew about what Amy did to Erin. But before he could finish, the door swung open. Erin's father pushed her wheel chair through the door. Erin didn't wait for him to get her close to the bed. She jumped from the chair leaping into the hospital bed with Charles. Charles grimaced once again, but was so glad to see Erin that he wrapped his arms around her as they embraced. Erin cried tears of joy.

"I didn't think that I would ever get a chance to see you again!" she exclaimed.

"I'm so sorry this happened to you," Charles stated.

Mocha, Billy, and Erin's parents quietly exited the room. They wanted to give the newly reunited couple some privacy.

3 2

MOCHA

*T*rue to form, William followed through on his threats to fire Mocha and kick Billy out of the family's company. Billy was amused and didn't let his fathers' temper tantrum faze him one bit. He and Mocha decided that their love was stronger than one man's attempt to break them apart.

William sent a certified letter to both Billy and Mocha, detailing when they could come into the building to clean out their personal belongings from his offices. He had security to meet them at the entrance to the building. They escorted each of them to their offices. It was his father's way of trying to embarrass them even further than they had been already.

Neither of them complained. The security guards apologized to Mocha and Billy once they were out of earshot of William. They both graciously accepted the apologies and informed them that they understood that they were only doing their jobs.

Billy didn't have much to collect. Most of the things in his office had been placed there by his secretary, who ordered all of the décor using the Baldwin Budget. He needed only a very small box for a few pictures and trophies.

Mocha had a bit a more to collect than Billy. She had pictures, plaques, gifts, and mementos that she had collected over the past six years, but that wasn't what she most wanted to collect from her office. She logged into her computer and began transferring her files. An hour later Mocha was engrossed in several files that she stumbled upon. She didn't hear Billy when he walked into the room. He had to call her name before she realized that he was standing there. "You are not going to believe what I have found," Mocha stated. "Come over here and take a look at this."

Billy looked over the first page of the documents. His initial shock at reading his grandfathers' will was surreal to him. He missed his grandfather dearly. Billy was just getting into his teenage years when his grandfather died. Before he passed, they were like Batman and Robin. His grandfather took him everywhere with him.

The outing that he missed most was flying to New York every year to catch the Yankee's season opener. It had been the most exciting thing to a young Billy, who more than anything idolized his grandfather. He would get to miss school, fly on a private jet, and sit right behind home plate. Billy could smell the roasted peanuts as he took a few minutes to reminiscence about the good old days.

Mocha asked him if understood what this meant. Billy reached down scooping her into his arms. He swung her around the office. Mocha laughed.

BILLY

*B*illy couldn't believe what Mocha had uncovered. He was glad that Mocha had decided to copy every file that she had ever worked on since she was hired at Baldwin six years ago. It was time consuming, but worth it. She wanted the files to help her compile a portfolio to send out to headhunters as she searched for new employment.

As she was searching through the database, several things seemed peculiar. She had seen several encrypted files before but the ones she recently stumbled upon hadn't been detectable the last time she was in the system. The dates listed were so old that she wondered why they hadn't been archived. The system was designed to filter out files once they reached the five year mark. Once that happened, there was a department in the building that. It took some finagling, but she was finally able to break through the firewall that housed the hidden secret of the decade.

Billy walked into his father's office with Mocha by his side. He had asked his mother to join them. She was already there. His father was grumbling as usual, complaining that he didn't have time for this impromptu meeting.

"Mocha and I are starting our own company. We expect to have

M&B Enterprises up and running within the next couple of months," Billy informed. Although he and Mocha had never spoken about starting their own company, he wanted to really stick it to his father and piss him off. We are also taking all the clients with us that we brokered into this company. William didn't speak initially. Neither did Billy. It was a classic cat and mouse game. William broke first.

"And just how do you plan on starting a company? I am not giving you a dime of my money to pour into a company that you and your mistress will run into the ground," William scolded.

"See, those are the type of comments that make me want to knock your head off," Billy threatened.

"You will not talk to me like that, boy," William feigned.

"I am not a boy and Mocha is not my mistress. She is my fiancé, and by next year, she will be Mrs. William Baldwin, III," Billy stated. Nancy smiled. She loved that her son had found his soul mate. Mocha was a lovely young woman. She had stated so on many occasion after meeting her a few years ago. Mocha was one of the few women in the company that Nancy was sure hadn't slept with William. She wanted her son to be happy, and from what she could tell, he was elated.

"Dad, a mistress would be Chloe, or Asha, or Valentina; or every other secretary that you've had over the past 40 years."

"Billy!" his mother exclaimed. She knew her husband could be an asshole, but she hadn't raised her son to be disrespectful to his elders.

"What has gotten into you? You have never spoken this way to your father. I support you and Mocha, but I will not allow you to speak disrespectfully to your father," Nancy proclaimed.

Nancy was really trying to save face. She didn't want anyone to know that she knew William was cheating on her all these years and had just decided to accept it.

"Mother, please stop with your blind loyalty to this man. He has never been worthy of your love. Dad you asked about our funding? I have to tell you, you did a heck of a job hiding the contents of grandpa's will, but not good enough. You see, this beautiful, chocolate woman right here, my beautiful African queen, uncovered all of your hidden secrets," Billy teased.

"Mother, your dad, my grandfather, had very little faith in your selection as a life mate. He doubted his ability to run this company, and he doubted his ability to love you the way you needed to be loved. Therefore, he put provisions into his will. Provisions that you were never made aware of because he and his best friend chose to hide them from you, the first thing being that he could not change the name of this company. Baldwin Enterprises should still be Newman Enterprises. Mother, upon my graduation day, after receiving my MBA, grandpa willed the company to me. Dad continued to operate as Senior Chief Executive Officer when he no longer had the authority to do so. To keep this a secret safe, he manufactured documents requesting my signature, then he would use software to transfer it to the documents he needed in order to keep the company running, Billy revealed.

"If it weren't for Mocha, he would have carried this secret to the grave. You see Dad, the real question becomes, do I let you keep running Baldwin Enterprises for me, or do I kick you out of the company flat on your ass? I was prepared to promote Mocha to your position, but being the person that she is, she convinced me not to do that. She realizes that, of course, you have worked hard to put Baldwin at the top of the Forbes list and actually proved grandpa wrong. You can run this company successfully. So, we are going to allow you to continue to do that, but we will be watching your every move. Every decision comes through us," Billy affirmed.

"But since neither I nor my mate can stand to be around you, we are branching out to form M&B Enterprises under the Baldwin umbrella. You can either accept our generous offer or retire. It's your choice," Billy quipped.

EPILOGUE

BILLY AND MOCHA

Billy and Mocha's wedding was the social event of the year. Everyone from Baldwin was invited to the wedding. Noticeably absent was William Baldwin. His grudge against his son and daughter in-law ran deep. In his eyes, his only son had committed the ultimate betrayal and disrespect. William refused to even broach the subject with his wife. She had implored him to come to the wedding. He refused. Billy and Mocha allowed their mothers and sisters to handle all of the arrangements. The Chateau Polonez was chosen as the venue for both the wedding and reception. The Chateau Polonez is tucked away in the forests of Northwest Houston.

The design was a European style venue that featured faux painted walls and vaulted ceilings throughout. The dramatic double staircase entry led to a beautiful grand ballroom. The venue was located on five acres of naturally wooded and manicured gardens. Mocha was pleased with every detail that was planned out for her special day.

Mocha's gown was, by far, the prettiest that any of the guests had ever seen. It was custom made and designed with Mocha in mind. Each piece of lace and frill had been hand-stitched to ensure its' uniqueness.

The gown was a custom-made Givenchy creation, which featured long lace sleeves and strategic sheer panels. It was a form-fitting silhouette that accented her curvaceous frame perfectly. She wore her hair up with a few cascading curls dangling down her back. The flowing veil covered much of her face and matched her dress. Billy also wore a Givenchy original. It was designed to coordinate with the bridal gown.

The bridal party included the couple's sisters, Charles, and Mocha's brother-in-law. The bridal party dresses were two varying Givenchy designs that accented each woman's attributes. The groomsmen tuxedos matched Billy's.

Mocha's father escorted her down the aisle. He had no doubt in his mind that Billy loved and cared for his daughter as much as he did. Placing her with him for safekeeping would be his honor.

Billy and Mocha had chosen to follow the traditional exchanging of the vows. It was always Mocha's dream to state "until death do us part." She loved Billy enormously and the only way she would leave him would be if it was beyond her control. Billy mirrored her sentiments and agreed.

When it was time for the minister to ask the congregation, "if anyone feels this couple should not be united in Holy Matrimony, speak now, or forever hold your peace," Mocha's mind briefly shifted to Amy. She wondered if, by chance, she had found out about the wedding and would have an outburst at that very moment. Mocha breathed a sigh of relief when she heard the minister say, "I now pronounce you man and wife." Applause erupted throughout the venue as Billy placed a passionate kiss upon his brides' lips.

CHARLES AND ERIN

Erin's parent's finally decided that she was in good hands with Charles and flew back to Boston after making him promise to take very good care of their little girl. Although it had only been a short time that Charles had known Erin, he knew she was the one. Both had experienced much with love and lust in the past and were ready to settle down. Charles proposed. Erin accepted. Charles' proposal to Erin was equally as impressive as Billy's proposal had been to Mocha. Charles flew Erin and her parents to Dallas. He planned an extravagant dinner at the Wolfgang Puck Restaurant located atop the Reunion Tower. The rotating restaurant 73 stories above ground provided the perfect ambiance for what he had planned. Erin's parents had no clue of his intentions that night. While they were taking in the 360 degree view of the city, a small plane began circling the tower. The banner in tow read "Erin Will You Marry Me." When she said yes, Charles and her parents were ecstatic. They have been engaged for three months. Like Mocha, Erin doesn't want a long engagement. She is planning to have her wedding two months after Billy and Mocha's wedding.

WILLIAM AND NANCY

*William couldn't take the fact that he still had to answer to Mocha and
Billy when it was all said and done. He decided to retire. William
received a severance package that ensured that he would never have to
work again. Billy also allowed for him and Nancy to receive a monthly
stipend. While his views were totally different than those of his father,
Billy would never allow his parents to be desolate. He knew his father
loved him, but he refused to be controlled by him. Nancy went vacationing without William every chance she got. She couldn't stand being
cooped up with him daily. On each trip that she took, she'd take the
love of her life. It was during these escapades that she was the happiest
that she had ever been in her entire life. It was no surprise to Billy that
whenever his mom was out of town vacationing, so was his housekeeper Melvin. Nancy was raised to believe that once you were
married you stay married. She had no intention of divorcing her
husband. She also had no intention of discontinuing her relationship
with her lover. Occasionally, she felt bad about her extra-marital affair,
but soon would remember how many times William had cheated on her.
Melvin was the first and only person that she had ever slept with,
besides William. She felt that her transgressions in no way matched*

his. If they each did a tally, she still had many more years with Melvin before she would catch up to William's infidelity.

AMY

Amy was beside herself. She considered herself better than Houdini. She had mastered the great escape once again. After leaving Houston, she cut her long brunette tresses. She now sported a short blonde pixie cut. She dropped the extra weight that she had put on to conceal Ambrosia. Now she was fitting in with the beach babes at Malibu.

When she was shopping for clothes in Arizona, the Beverly Hillbillies rerun was playing on the television behind the counter. She took it to heart when she heard California is the place you ought to be, so she that's where she went. It was so far away from Texas that she decided to go back to using Ambrosia. It was more of a California-sounding name than Amy. She doubted anyone would look for her so far away. Baldwin Towers and all the people associated with it were but a distant memory to her.

The first thing Amy did when she arrived in California was to walk the streets of West Hollywood. She needed to get some new identification cards so that she could start looking for a job. The cash she had saved when she was in Texas was almost half gone. She really didn't want to get another job. It had almost cost her freedom being in such close proximity to the same people every day.

Amy pulled her car into the gas station on the Sunset Strip. She loved this city. The warmth of this day had her rethinking looking for a job. Why be cooped up in an office when you could be out taking in the rays? Amy finished filling up her gas tank. She was pulling out of the station when a Black Land Rover Range Rover slammed into the front drivers' side of Amy's car.

The driver of the Range Rover jumped out and ran to Amy's car. She asked if she was alright. Amy nodded her head yes, as she was still a little dazed from the impact. The driver apologized, saying she had only looked down for a moment to answer her ringing cellular phone. Amy was hoping that the woman would just shut up. She was babbling a mile a minute.

When Amy finally looked into the woman's face, she recognized her immediately. Although she couldn't remember from which show, she knew that she was an actress on one of the daytime talk shows. Amy wracked her brain trying to figure out which show she had seen the woman on.

"Who are you?" Amy had finally asked.

"I'm sorry," the woman responded, "my name is Taylor Thomas-Thornton.

Bingo, Amy thought. She's on that morning talk show with that African American dude.

Taylor gave Amy all of her insurance information. She ensured Amy that she would take care of all of her expenses.

Amy's brain started clicking. This was just the connection she needed. She had just made up her mind. She would not be looking for a job. At least not in the traditional sense, but she was about to work over Mrs. Taylor Thomas-Thornton.

"Welcome to Hollywood," She said to herself.

Text ROYALTY to 42828 to get a notification when PART TWO comes out!

Royalty Publishing House is now accepting manuscripts from aspiring or experienced urban romance authors!

WHAT MAY PLACE YOU ABOVE THE REST:

Heroes who are the ultimate book bae: strong-willed, maybe a little rough around the edges but willing to risk it all for the woman he loves.

Heroines who are the ultimate match: the girl next door type, not perfect - has her faults but is still a decent person. One who is willing to risk it all for the man she loves.

The rest is up to you! Just be creative, think out of the box, keep it sexy and intriguing!

If you'd like to join the Royal family, send us the first 15K words (60 pages) of your completed manuscript to submissions@royaltypublish-inghouse.com

LIKE OUR PAGE!

Be sure to LIKE our Royalty Publishing House page on Facebook!